PRACTICE BOOK

Grade 1

Macmillan/McGraw-Hill

New York • Farmington

Macmillan/McGraw-Hill
A Division of The **McGraw·Hill** Companies

Macmillan/McGraw-Hill
1221 Avenue of the Americas
New York, New York 10020

Printed in the United States of America

ISBN 0-02-181185-7/ 1

15 16 17 18 DBH 05 04 03

CONTENTS

LEVEL 1

READ ALL ABOUT IT!

LEVEL 2

OUT AND ABOUT

Bet You Can't

Coco Can't Wait!

Down by the Bay

Jasper's Beanstalk

SOMETHING NEW

An Egg Is an Egg

Whose Baby?

Everything Grows

White Rabbit's Color Book

LEVEL 4

UNIT I: TAKE A CLOSER LOOK

UNIT 2: SURPRISES ALONG THE WAY

LEVEL 5

UNIT 1: LET'S PRETEND

UNIT 2: TRUE-BLUE FRIENDS

CAR WORDS

Write **c** if the picture name begins with the same sound as **car**.

1. _____

2. _____

3. _____

4. _____

5. _____

6. _____

7. _____

8. _____

9. _____

10. _____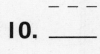

 10 Level 1
Initial Consonant /k/ *c*

Extension: Have children think of words that begin with the same sound as **car**. Then have them draw a picture to go with each word.

1

WAGON WORDS

Circle the picture whose name begins with the same sound as **wagon**.

1.

2.

3.

4.

5.

6.

7.

8.

9.

10.

Extension: Have children look in books and magazines for pictures whose names begin with the same sound as **wagon**.

Level 1
Initial Consonant /w/ *w*

10

Name: _____   Date: _____

PENCIL WORDS

Write the letter **p** to complete the word.

Circle the picture the word names.

1. _____ an

 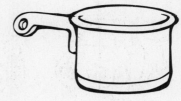

2. _____ ig

3. _____ en

4. _____ in

5. _____ up

WHAT'S WRONG?

Look at each picture and circle the thing that does not belong.

1.

2.

3.

4.

5.

Extension: Have children draw a picture of something that would fit in each scene.

Macmillan/McGraw-Hill

Name: _____   Date: _____

FIRST, NEXT, LAST

Number the pictures 1, 2, 3 to show what happened first, next, and last. The first one is done for you.

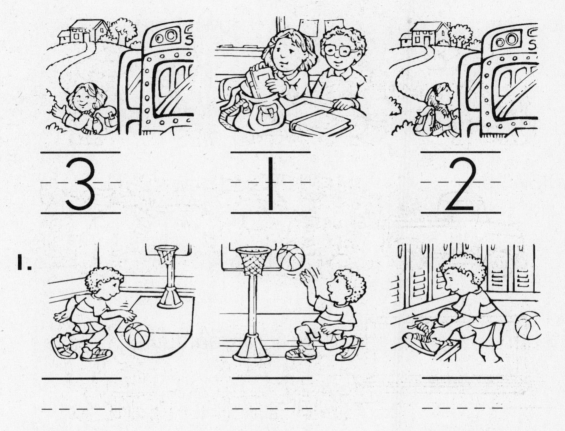

3   1   2

1.

_____   _____   _____

2.

_____   _____   _____

Macmillan/McGraw-Hill

Level 1
ORGANIZE INFORMATION: Sequence of Events

Extension: Have children draw a picture of something that could happen next for each row.

5

WHAT I SAW!

Circle the animals you saw in the story *I Went Walking*. Color the story animals.

1. black cat

2. brown horse

3. yellow lion

4. red cow

5. red hen

6. green duck

7. green bird

8. yellow dog

Extension: Ask children to use the pictures they circled to retell the story.

Level 1
Story Comprehension

8

Macmillan/McGraw-Hill

I WENT WALKING

I	What	see

Write a word from the box to complete each question. Circle the picture that answers the question.

1. _____ _ _ _ _ _ _ _ _ _ can I see?

2. What can _____ _ _ _ _ _ _ _ _ _ see?

3. What can I _____ _ _ _ _ _ _ _ _ _ ?

4. _____ _ _ _ _ _ _ _ _ _ can I see?

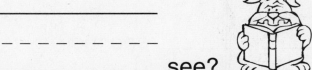

5. What can _____ _ _ _ _ _ _ _ _ _ see?

5

Level 1
High Utility Words

Extension: Have children make up a new question for each vocabulary word.

7

Name: _____   Date: _____

I WENT WALKING

you	me	saw

Write a word from the box to complete each sentence.

1. I _____ you.

2. Did _____ see me?

3. Can you see _____ ?

4. I saw _____ in the box.

5. I _____ the cat!

Macmillan/McGraw-Hill

8

Extension: Have children write a new sentence for each word in the box.

Level 1
High-Utility Words

5

Name: _____   Date: _____

I WENT WALKING

what	I	me	saw	you	see

Write a word from the box to complete each sentence.

_____

1. _____ am a cat.

_____

2. Are _____ a duck?

_____

3. Did I _____ you on the cow?

_____

4. Did you see _____ I saw?

_____

5. You and I _____ a pig sit on _____.

Macmillan/McGraw-Hill

6 Level 1
High-Utility Words

Extension: Have children draw pictures of things they can see on a farm.

9

FAT CAT

Write two **-at** words to complete each sentence.

fat   cat   bat   rat   mat

_____ _____
1. This is a _____ _____.

_____
2. This is a _____
_____
for a _____.

_____ _____
3. This is a _____ _____.

_____
4. This is a _____
_____
for a _____.

Extension: Have children think of words that rhyme with **cat.** Then have them draw pictures to go with the words.

Level 1
Short Vowels and Phonograms /a/ -at

8

Name: _____   Date: _____

Fox Words

Write the letter **f**. Then draw lines from the letter to the pictures whose names begin with the same sound as **fox**.

1. _____
_____
_____

2. _____
_____
_____

3. _____
_____
_____

4. _____
_____
_____

5. _____
_____
_____

6. _____
_____
_____
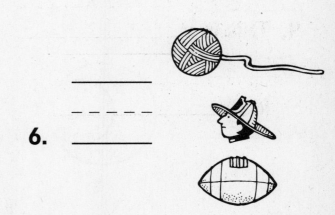

Extension: Have children tell a story about a fox, using words that begin with **f**, such as **fence**, **food**, **funny**, **fit**, and **fine**.

Name: _____   Date: _____

RABBIT WORDS

Write the letter **r** next to each picture whose name begins with the same sound as **rabbit.**

1. _____

2. _____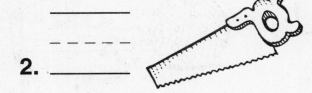

3. _____

4. _____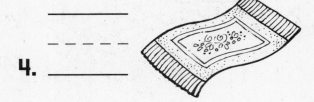

5. _____

6. _____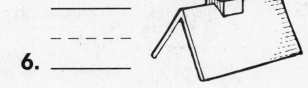

7. _____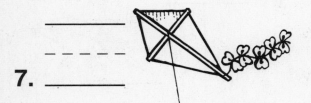

8. _____

9. _____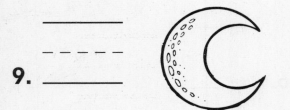

10. _____

Extension: Have children think of words that begin with the same sound as rabbit. Then have them draw a picture to go with each word.

Level 1
Initial Consonants /r/ r

10

Yo-Yo Words

Circle the word that names the picture.

Write the letter that stands for the beginning sound.

1.    barn
   yarn   _____

2.    yard
   card   _____

3.    bell
   yell   _____

4.    dawn
   yawn   _____

5.    back
   yak   _____

Level 1
Initial Consonant /y/ y

Extension: Have children think of words that begin with the same
sound as yo-yo. Help them make a list of the words.

13

Macmillan/McGraw-Hill

MORE THAN ONE

Write the word that names each picture.

cat	pig	hen	dogs	cows
dog	cow	cats	pigs	hens

1. _____

2. _____

3. _____

4. _____

5. _____

6. _____

7. _____

8. _____

9. _____

10. _____

Extension: Have children draw pictures of words that mean more than one. Help them label each picture.

Level 1
Plurals

10

Macmillan/McGraw-Hill

BIG IDEAS!

Circle the sentence that tells about the picture.

1.

The pigs live here.

The cats live here.

2.

I see the cat.

I see the rain.

3.

The dog likes the rain.

The cat likes the rain.

4.

Ducks play here.

Cows play here.

5.

Cats play here.

Mice play here.

Macmillan/McGraw-Hill

5

Level 1
**ORGANIZE INFORMATION: Main Idea
and Supporting Details**

Extension: Ask children to look for pictures that show people or places.
Then have them tell the main idea of each picture.

15

RAIN

Circle the words that tell about the story. Then color the picture.

1.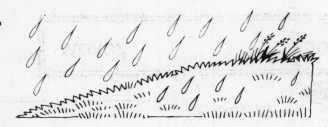

green grass

blue grass

2.

black car

red car

3.

orange flowers

gray flowers

4.

blue house

white house

5.

red trees

green trees

Extension: Have children use the items on the page to retell that part of the story.

Level 1
Story Comprehension

5

RAIN

Circle the color word that fits the picture.

Write the word.

blue	black	yellow

1.   black
     blue

_____

2.   yellow
     black

_____

3.   blue
     yellow

_____

4.   black
     yellow

_____

5.   black
     blue

_____

Macmillan/McGraw-Hill

Level 1
High Utility Words

Extension: Ask children to make color cards for **black, yellow,** and **blue** and place the cards in a row. Ask them to point to a color you name.

17

RAIN

Write the color word from the story. Then color the picture.

| white | red | brown | green |

1.

_____

a _____ horse

2.

_____

a _____ rooster

3.

_____

a _____ bear

4.

_____

a _____ leaf

5.

_____

a _____ hen

Extension: Have children make color cards for **white, red, brown,** and **green.** Ask them to hold up the card for the color you name.

Level 1
High-Utility Words

5

Macmillan/McGraw-Hill

Name: _____ Date: _____

RAIN

Read the words.

Color the picture.

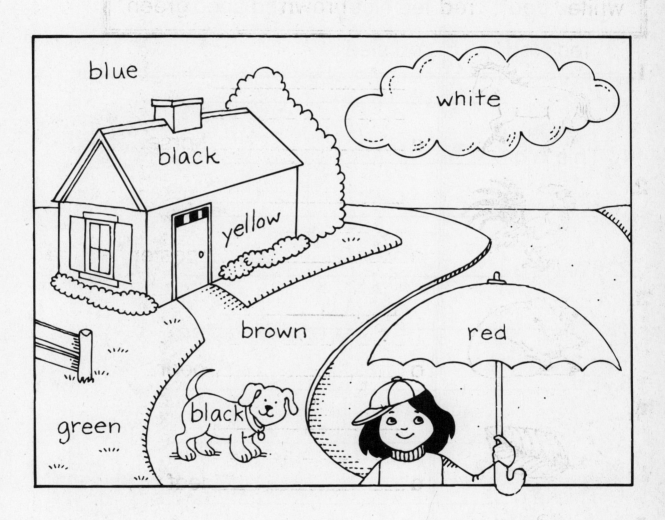

8 Level 1
High-Utility Words

Extension: Have children use the set of color cards from pages 17 and 18. Ask them to match the cards to the items in the picture.

RED, RED!

Write the words to complete the sentences. Color the things that are red.

red bed	led Ned	red shed
fed Ned	red sled	

1. This is a _____.

2. This is a _____.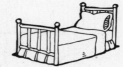

3. Ed _____.

4. This is a _____.

5. Ed _____.

Extension: Have children write or dictate sentences using the **-ed** words on the page.

Level 1
Short Vowels and Phonograms /e/-ed

5

Macmillan/McGraw-Hill

QUIET WORDS

Write the letters **qu** next to each picture whose name begins with the same sound as **queen.**

1. _____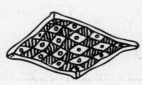

2. _____

3. _____

4. _____

5. _____

6. _____

7. _____

8. _____

9. _____

10. _____

Macmillan/McGraw-Hill

10
Level 1
Initial Consonants /kw/ *qu*

Extension: Ask children to look in magazines for words that begin with the letters **qu.** Have them copy the words, and then help them read each word.

21

Name: _____   Date: _____

IN ORDER

Number the sentences from 1 to 3 to show what happens first, next, and last.

1.
        I got to school.

        I got on the bus.

        I got up.

2.
        I went out.

        I played in the rain.

        I got my coat.

22 **Extension:** Ask children to retell each event in a story. Remind them to keep the steps in order.

Level 1
ORGANIZE INFORMATION: Sequence of Events

2

ADD -S

Add the letter **-s** to each word. Write the new word.

1. hat + s

_____

2. duck + s

_____

3. girl + s

_____

4. boy + s

_____

5. sled + s

_____

5

Level 1
Plurals

Extension: Say words that identify one object (car). Have children give the word that means more than one (cars).

23

Macmillan/McGraw-Hill

Name: _____   Date: _____

BALL WORDS

Write the letter **b** to complete each picture name that begins with the same sound as **ball.**

1. _____ ib

2. _____ us

3. _____ an

4. _____ ed

5. _____ ox

6. _____ at

7. _____ at

8. _____ ell

9. _____ all

10. _____ ox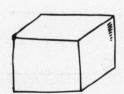

Extension: Have children find pictures whose names begin with the same sound as **ball.** Ask volunteers to show their pictures and tell what they found.

24

Level 1
Initial Consonants /b/ *b*
10

Macmillan/McGraw-Hill

Name: _____ Date: _____

HAT WORDS

Write the letter **h** next to each picture whose name begins with the same sound as **hat.**

1. _____

2. _____

3. _____

4. _____

5. _____

6. _____

7. _____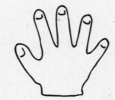

8. _____

9. _____

10. _____

10

Level 1
Initial Consonants /h/ *h*

Extension: Have children draw pictures of items whose names begin with the same sound as **hat** and are things that are found in a house.

25

Macmillan/McGraw-Hill

Name: _____ Date: _____

FIVE LITTLE DUCKS

Put an X on the duck that went away.

1. One duck went away

2. And one duck went away

3. And one duck went away

4. And one duck went away

5. And one duck went away.

Draw a picture to show what happened next.

26 **Extension:** Have children tell about the picture they drew.

Level 1
Story Comprehension 6

Macmillan/McGraw-Hill

UP AND DOWN

Write the word that means the opposite.

little	went	out	over

1. big _____

2. in _____

3. under _____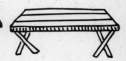

4. came _____

Macmillan/McGraw-Hill

☐/4 Level 1
High-Utility Words

Extension: Ask children to give sentences using words that are opposites.

27

Name: _____   Date: _____

CHOOSE A WORD

| and | said | went |

Write the word that rhymes.

1.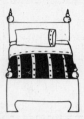

_____

- - - - - - - - - - - -

2.

_____

- - - - - - - - - - - -

3.

_____

- - - - - - - - - - - -

Write a word from the box to complete each sentence.

_____

- - - - - - - - - -

4. One duck _____ away.

_____

- - - - - - - - - -

5. "The duck went away," _____ Mother Duck.

_____

- - - - - - - - - -

6. Mother Duck _____ the ducks came home.

28   **Extension:** Ask volunteers to create new sentences for the vocabulary words.

Level 1
High-Utility Words

6

Macmillan/McGraw-Hill

SOLVE THE PUZZLES

Write the words to complete the puzzles.

little   went   out   over   and   said

1. begins with **o**

2. begins with **o**

3. begins with **l**

4. begins with **a**

5. begins with **s**

6. begins with **w**

6 Level 1
High-Utility Words

Extension: Have children dictate or write a sentence for each vocabulary word.

29

CUT A NUT

Write a word to complete each sentence.

nut	shut	cut	rut	hut

1. This is a _____.

2. Please _____ the door.

3. I can _____ the string.

4. The car is in the _____.

5. The _____ is little.

Extension: Have children choose a word and draw a picture. Help them write a sentence to tell about their picture.

Level 1
Short Vowels and Phonograms /u/ -ut

5

Macmillan/McGraw-Hill

Name: _____ Date: _____

WHAT HAPPENED?

Look at the first picture.
Circle the picture that shows what happened next.

1.

2.

3.

4.

5.

Macmillan/McGraw-Hill

Level 1
ORGANIZE INFORMATION: Cause and Effect

Extension: Have children draw a pair of pictures to show an example of cause and effect.

31

5

Name: _____ Date: _____

The Chick and the Duckling
PHONICS: INITIAL
CONSONANTS /d/ d

DUCK WORDS

Write the letter **d** to complete the word.

Circle the picture the word names.

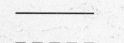
1. _____ uck

_____
2. _____ og

_____
3. _____ esk

_____
4. _____ oor

_____
5. _____ oll

Extension: Have children find magazine pictures of things whose names begin with the same sound as **duck**. Then have them show and tell about their pictures.

Level 1
Initial Consonants /d/ d

5

Macmillan/McGraw-Hill

Name: _____ Date: _____

The Chick and the Duckling
PHONICS: Initial
Consonants /n/ *n*

Net Words

Write the letter **n.**

Draw a line to the picture whose name begins with the same sound as **net.**

1. _____ _____

2. _____ _____

3. _____ _____

4. _____ _____

5. _____ _____

6. _____ _____

6 Level 1
Initial Consonants /n/ *n*

Extension: Have children think of words that begin with the same sound as **net.** Then have them draw a picture to go with each word.

33

Macmillan/McGraw-Hill

Name: _____ Date: _____

The Chick and the Duckling
PHONICS: INITIAL
CONSONANTS /t/ t

TURTLE WORDS

Write the letter **t** next to each picture whose name begins with the same sound as **turtle**.

1. _____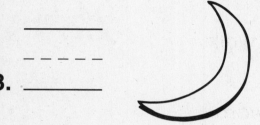

2. _____

3. _____

4. _____

5. _____

6. _____

7. _____

8. _____

Extension: Have children write a sentence using two words that begin with the same sound as **turtle**.

Level 1
Initial Consonants /t/ t

8

Macmillan/McGraw-Hill

THE CHICK AND THE DUCKLING

Circle the sentences that tell what happened in the story.

The chick and the duckling take a walk.

The chick and the duckling get a worm.

The chick and the duckling get a cat.

The chick and the duckling get a butterfly.

The chick and the duckling go for a swim.

The chick can swim.

The duckling can swim.

Macmillan/McGraw-Hill

5

Level 1
Story Comprehension

Extension: Have children retell the story using the sentences they circled.

Name: _____   Date: _____

THE CHICK AND THE DUCKLING

Read the words in the box.

not	am	found

Draw a line to match each sentence with a picture.

1. I found a cat.

2. I found a chick.

3. I am a duckling.

4. I am a chick.

5. I am not big.

6. I am not little.

Extension: Have children circle the vocabulary word in each sentence
on the page.

Macmillan/McGraw-Hill

THE CHICK AND THE DUCKLING

Write a word from the box to complete each sentence.

going	too	for

1. I will look _____ the duck.

2. I will look _____ the chick.

3. I am _____ to swim.

4. Are you _____ to swim?

5. I want to swim, _____ .

Extension: Have children write a sentence for each vocabulary word, and then illustrate their sentences.

Name: _____   Date: _____

THE CHICK AND THE DUCKLING

Draw a line to complete each sentence.

1. Help me look ___ the duck.   not

2. You can help, ___.   for

3. The duck is ___ big.   too

4. We ___ the duck.   going

5. The duck is ___ to swim.   am

6. I ___ going to swim, too.   found

Draw a picture to show one thing that happens in the story.

Extension: Have children make word cards for the vocabulary words. Have them place the cards in a pile and take turns drawing a card and reading the word.

38

Level 1
High-Utility Words

6

Macmillan/McGraw-Hill

The Chick and the Duckling
PHONICS: SHORT VOWELS
AND PHONOGRAMS /o/ -ot

Name: _____ Date: _____

HOT, HOT!

Write the word that names the picture.

| dot | cot | hot | lot | pot | tot |

1.

_____

- - - - - - - - - - -

a black _____

2.

_____

- - - - - - - - - - -

a _____ of toys

3.

_____

- - - - - - - - - - -

one big _____

4.

_____

- - - - - - - - - - -

a _____

5.

_____

- - - - - - - - - - -

very _____

6.

_____

- - - - - - - - - - -

little _____

Extension: Help children use two of the **-ot** words to complete this sentence: This is a _____.

Macmillan/McGraw-Hill

Name: _____   Date: _____

GOAT WORDS

Write the letter **g** if the name of the picture begins
with the same sound as **goat.**

1. _____

2. _____

3. _____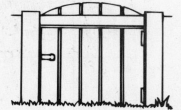

4. _____

5. _____

6. _____

7. _____

8. _____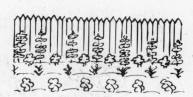

9. _____

10. _____

Extension: Give a clue for a word that begins with the same sound as
goat. (Example: a musical instrument) Ask children to guess the word
that fits the clue. (guitar)

40

Level 1
Initial Consonants /g/ g

10

Macmillan/McGraw-Hill

Name: _____   Date: _____

Mouse Words

Draw lines from the letter **m** to the pictures whose names begin with the same sound as **mouse.**

1.

m

2.

m

3.

m

4.

m

5.

m

6.

m

6

Level 1
Initial Consonants /m/ m

Extension: Have children write the letter **m** and draw two more pictures that begin with the same sound as **mouse.**

SEAL WORDS

Circle the pictures in each row whose names begin
with the same sound as **seal**.

1.

2.

3.

4.

5.

Extension: Have children think of words that begin with the same
sound as **seal.** Write the words in a list on chart paper.

Level 1
Initial Consonants /s/ *s*

10

Macmillan/McGraw-Hill

-ED ACTION

Draw a line to the word that completes the sentence.

1. Tom ___ at the toys.   played

Jan ___ with the toys.   looked

2. Ivan ___ with Bob to school.   talked

Lisa ___ on the phone.   walked

3. Juan ___ the wagon out of the road.   pushed

Maria ___ up and down.   jumped

4. Sara ___ at the lake.   pulled

Jose ___ on the rope.   fished

4

Level 1
STRUCTURAL CLUES: Inflectional
Endings -ed

Extension: Point to one of the words in the second column and ask children to use the word in a sentence.

43

WHERE IS IT?

Look at the picture.

Write a word from the box to complete the sentence.

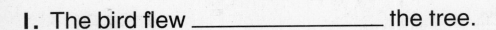

over	under	across	on	in

1. The bird flew _____ the tree.

2. The dog ran _____ the yard.

3. The fox sat _____ the tree.

4. The cat hid _____ the box.

5. The hen sat _____ the hat.

Extension: Point to an object in the room and have children use words such as **on**, **over**, and **under** to tell where the object is.

Level 1
ORGANIZE INFORMATION: Spatial Relationships

5

Macmillan/McGraw-Hill

Name: _____   Date: _____

WHY?

Look at the pictures. The first picture in each row shows something that happened.

Circle the picture that shows why it happened.

1.

2.

3.

4.

5.

Level 1
ORGANIZE INFORMATION: Cause and Effect

5

Macmillan/McGraw-Hill

Extension: Have children draw pictures to show cause and effect events.

45

THE GOOD BAD CAT

Circle **good cat** or **bad cat** to tell the story.

1. ran under the chair

good cat

bad cat

2. ran over the game

good cat

bad cat

3. jumped on the table

good cat

bad cat

4. saw a mouse

good cat

bad cat

5. got the mouse out of the house

good cat

bad cat

46 **Extension:** Have children make up a story about a cat.

Level 1
Story Comprehension

5

Macmillan/McGraw-Hill

Name: _____ Date: _____

THE GOOD BAD CAT

Write a word from the box to tell about the picture.

good	bad	under

1.  _____

2.  _____

3.  _____

4.  _____

5.  _____

5

Level 1
High-Utility Words

Extension: Have children draw a picture for each vocabulary word.

47

THE GOOD BAD CAT

Write the word from the box to complete each sentence.

on	across	so

_____
- - - - - - - - - -

1. Go _____ the road.

_____
- - - - - - - - - -

2. Put it _____ the table.

_____
- - - - - - - - - -

3. I ran fast and _____ did you.

_____
- - - - - - - - - -

4. Put a top _____ it.

_____
- - - - - - - - - -

5. We can swim _____.

48   **Extension:** Ask children to write a sentence for each vocabulary word.

Level 1
High-Utility Words

5

Macmillan/McGraw-Hill

Name: _____ Date: _____

THE GOOD BAD CAT

Find a word in the box that matches each clue.
Write the word in the boxes.

| across | good | so |
| bad | on | under |

1. something you like

2. something you don't like

3. not off

4. walk _____ the road

5. not over

6. rhymes with **no**

Macmillan/McGraw-Hill

Extension: Have children work with partners to create sentences for the vocabulary words.

Name: _____   Date: _____

HID WORDS

Choose a word from the box to complete each
sentence. Write the word.

kid	did	slid	hid	lid

_____

1. I _____ from you.

_____

2. A _____ ran fast.

_____

3. You _____ good work.

_____

4. The _____ was on the pan.

_____

5. I _____ down the hill.

Extension: Have children draw pictures for each of the **-id** words on
the page.

Level 1
5

Short Vowels and Phonograms /i/ -id

Macmillan/McGraw-Hill

JET WORDS

Write the letter **j** to complete the word.

Circle the picture the word names.

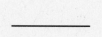
1. _____ eep

2. _____ ug

3. _____ ar

4. _____ ump

5. _____ acks

Macmillan/McGraw-Hill

5

Level 1
Initial Consonants /j/ *j*

Extension: Have children think of other words that begin with the same
sound as **jet**.

51

KITE WORDS

Write the letter **k** next to each picture whose name begins with the same sound as **kite.**

1. _____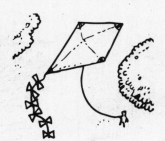

2. _____

3. _____

4. _____

5. _____

6. _____

7. _____

8. _____

Extension: Have children name other words that begin with the same sound as **kite.**

Level 1
Initial Consonants /k/ *k*

8

Macmillan/McGraw-Hill

Name: ____________________ Date: ____________________

TELL WHY

Look at the picture.
Circle the picture that shows why it happened.

1.   

2.   

3.   

4.   

Extension: Have children tell about the pictures they circled and identify the cause and effect.

LOTS AND LOTS

Write the word from the box that names the picture.

net	cot	pen	mop	bed
nets	cots	pens	mops	beds

1. _____
   _____

2. _____
   _____

3. _____
   _____

4. _____
   _____

5. _____
   _____

6. _____
   _____

7. _____
   _____

8. _____
   _____

9. _____
   _____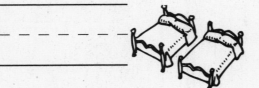

10. _____
    _____

54
Extension: Name a noun, and have children tell the plural form of the word.

Level 1
STRUCTURAL CLUES: Plurals

10

Macmillan/McGraw-Hill

LION WORDS

Write the word that names the picture.

log	leg	lips	lid
lock	leaf	lamp	lamb

1. _____

2. _____

3. _____

4. _____

5. _____

6. _____

7. _____

8. _____

8
Level 1
Initial Consonants /l/ *l*

Extension: Have children make up sentences for three of the **l** words.

SORT IT!

Circle the picture that does not belong in each group.

1.

2.

3.

4.

5.

6.

Extension: Have children name objects that fit into these groups: pets, toys, clothing, books.

Level 1
ORGANIZE INFORMATION: Categories   6

Name: Date:

MY FRIENDS

Draw a line from what I learned to the friend that taught me.

1. walk

2. kick

3. jump

4. sing

5. climb

6. read

7. run

8. hide

9. march

10. nap

10 Level 1
Story Comprehension

Extension: Have children retell the story using the pictures of the animals on the page.

57

MY FRIENDS

Write each word under the picture it tells about.

jump	walk	play

1. _____
   - - - - - - - - - -

2. _____
   - - - - - - - - - -

3. _____
   - - - - - - - - - -

4. _____
   - - - - - - - - - -

5. _____
   - - - - - - - - - -

6. _____
   - - - - - - - - - -

Extension: Have children write a sentence that tells about each picture on the page.

Macmillan/McGraw-Hill

MY FRIENDS

Write a word from the box to complete each sentence.

| my | from | run |

_____

1. This is _____ pet.

_____

2. My pet can _____ .

_____

3. It can run _____ here to there.

_____

4. It can _____ across the yard.

_____

5. It can run _____ me to you.

_____

6. I like _____ pet.

6 Level 1
High-Utility Words

Extension: Ask children to draw pictures for the first three sentences on the page.

59

MY FRIENDS

Write a word from the box to complete each group of words. Draw a line from the group of words to the picture it tells about.

my	from	run
jump	play	

1. _____ dog

2. _____ a game

3. _____ down

4. home _____ school

5. _____ fast

Macmillan/McGraw-Hill

Extension: Have children write sentences using the phrases on the page.

CAP NAP WORDS

Write the word that names each picture.

nap	map	rap	lap	cap	clap

1. _____

2. _____

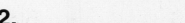

3. _____

4. _____

5. _____

6. _____

6   Level 1
Short Vowels and Phonograms /a/ -ap

Extension: Have children create sentences using any of the **-ap** words on the page.

61

CUMULATIVE VOCABULARY REVIEW

Look at the words in the box. Underline the word your teacher says.

1. what white went	**2.** saw and said	**3.** you yellow jump
4. me not on	**5.** blue black bad	**6.** red too run
7. brown green good	**8.** little walk play	**9.** out over across
10. under found for	**11.** am so my	**12.** cat bad the

Macmillan/McGraw-Hill

CUMULATIVE VOCABULARY REVIEW

Circle the word that tells about the picture.

1.

walk

jump

2.

play

sat

3.

run

found

4.

not

under

5.

over

what

6.

saw

run

Macmillan/McGraw-Hill

CUMULATIVE VOCABULARY REVIEW

Circle the word that goes on the line.

1. the _____ cat

little

what

2. give it to _____

went

me

3. run and _____

going

jump

4. _____ a game

play

said

5. _____ to school

walk

too

6. _____ my pet

black

found

7. a _____ sun

brown

yellow

8. _____ the door

run

out

CUMULATIVE VOCABULARY REVIEW

Underline the words that tell about the picture.
Write the words on the lines.

_____

- - - - - - - - - - - - - - - -

_____

1.

I walk　　　I run

_____

- - - - - - - - - - - - - - - -

_____

2.

went under　went across

_____

- - - - - - - - - - - - - - - -

_____

3.

saw a boy　　saw a girl

_____

- - - - - - - - - - - - - - - -

_____

4.

bad cat　　　good cat

_____

- - - - - - - - - - - - - - - -

_____

5.

not black　　not little

Level 1
Cumulative Vocabulary Review

TELL WHAT HAPPENS

Look at the picture. Underline the sentence that tells what will happen.

1.

The cans fall.

She sees a car.

2.

The cat plays with the dog.

The cat runs away.

3.

The pins fall.

The pins play.

4.

The girl plays a game.

The girl goes to bed.

5.

The boy hits the ball.

The boy sits down.

Extension: Have children draw two pictures and write two sentences: one about a cause and one about an effect.

Level 2
ORGANIZE INFORMATION: Cause and Effect

5

Macmillan/McGraw-Hill

Name: _____ Date: _____

SHOWING MORE THAN ONE

Add the letter **s** to the word if the picture shows
more than one.

1. __dog__

2. __car__

3. __bike__

4. __doll__

5. __mitten__

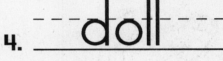
6. __hat__

7. __block__

8. __skate__

Macmillan/McGraw-Hill

8

Level 2
STRUCTURAL CLUES: Plurals

Extension: Ask children to draw pairs of pictures: one showing a
singular noun and one showing a plural noun. Have them label their
pictures.

67

BET YOU CAN'T

Circle the sentence that tells what each person said.

1.

I am cleaning up.

I found a yellow cat.

2.

It is bedtime.

I can lift it.

3.

I can't lift it.

Bet I can lift it.

4.

I am hiding.

I am in bed.

5.

I can't clean up.

I can clean up.

Extension: Ask children to draw three pictures that show what happened in the story.

Level 2
Story Comprehension

5

Macmillan/McGraw-Hill

BET YOU CAN'T

Underline the sentence that tells about the picture.

are	clean	why	it	can	away

1.

There are toys in the box.

I see a green dog.

2.

The hands are clean.

The hands are not clean.

3.

Is the cat little?

Why did the dog run away?

4.

It can eat grass.

It can't eat grass.

5.

She is going away.

She can't go away.

5

Level 2
High-Utility Words

Extension: Have children write a sentence about something they can do.

69

BET YOU CAN'T

Write the words from the box that complete the sentences.

| are | clean | Why | it | can | away |

_____
- - - - - - - - -
1. The dog will get _____.

_____   _____
- - - - - - - - -   - - - - - - - - -
2. _____ did the baby go _____?

_____
- - - - - - - - -
3. Where _____ the cats?

_____
- - - - - - - - -
4. He can see _____.

_____
- - - - - - - - -
5. It _____ jump away.

Extension: Direct children to write sentences in which they leave a
blank for a word that a classmate can fill in.

Level 2
High-Utility Words

6

Macmillan/McGraw-Hill

Name: _____   Date: _____

BET YOU CAN'T

Write a word from the box to complete each question. Circle the picture that answers the question.

are	clean	Why	it	can	away

1. What will _____ a car?

2. What will _____ want to eat?

3. What _____ a baby do?

4. What things _____ red?

5. What can jump _____?

6. _____ did it go away?

6 Level 2
High-Utility Words

Extension: Ask children to use words from the box to write questions for classmates to answer orally.

Jet Words

Circle the word that tells about the picture. Write the word.

1.    pet

jet

_____

- - - - - - - - - - - -

_____

2.    pet

met

_____

- - - - - - - - - - - -

_____

3. 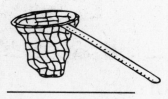   bet

net

_____

- - - - - - - - - - - -

_____

4.    get

set

_____

- - - - - - - - - - - -

_____

5.    let

wet

_____

- - - - - - - - - - - -

_____

6. 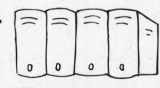   set

wet

_____

- - - - - - - - - - - -

_____

7.    net

vet

_____

- - - - - - - - - - - -

_____

8.    get

met

_____

- - - - - - - - - - - -

_____

Macmillan/McGraw-Hill

72   **Extension:** Invite children to tell a story about a pet or a jet.

Level 2
Short Vowels and Phonograms /e/ -et

8

CLOCK WORDS

Write the letters **cl** on the line if the name of the picture begins with the same sound as **clock.**

1. _____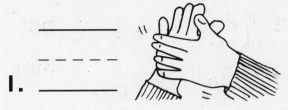

2. _____

3. _____

4. _____

5. _____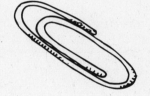

6. _____

7. _____

8. _____

9. _____

10. _____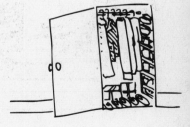

10 | Level 2
Consonant Blends /kl/ *cl*

Extension: Invite children to write sentences about three of the pictures that begin with the same sound as **clock.**

DOES IT BELONG?

Read the group name and the words. Write the words that belong in each group.

Animals

dog   house

tree   cat

_____

1. _____

_____

2. _____

People

dad   hat

grandma roof

_____

3. _____

_____

4. _____

Things with Wheels

book   car

bus   apple

_____

5. _____

_____

6. _____

Things to Put On

hat   sock

bike   cow

_____

7. _____

_____

8. _____

Extension: Have children choose a category and list as many words as possible that would belong in that category.

Level 2
ORGANIZE INFORMATION: Categories

8

7Macmillan/McGraw-Hill

Name: _____   Date: _____

WHERE IS IT?

Write the word from the box that completes each sentence.

across	over	under	in	out

1. The goat went _____ the hill.

2. The cat is _____ the bed.

3. It went _____ the road.

4. The fish is _____ the water.

5. The dog went _____.

5

Level 2
**ORGANIZE INFORMATION: Spatial
Relationships**

Extension: Ask children to write a sentence for each word in the box.

75

HOT WORDS

Look at the picture. Read the question. Write the answer. Use one of the underlined words.

I. Is this a <u>pot</u> or a <u>tot</u>?

2. Is this a <u>spot</u> or a <u>lot</u>?

3. Is this a <u>dot</u> or a <u>cot</u>?

4. Is this a <u>lot</u> or a <u>tot</u>?

5. Is this a <u>knot</u> or a <u>dot</u>?

76   **Extension:** Invite children to write sentences for the words they wrote.

Level 2

Short Vowels and Phonograms /o/ -ot

5

Macmillan/McGraw-Hill

Name: _____   Date: _____

CAN YOU DO IT?

Write **1, 2,** or **3** to show the order in which things take place.

1.

 _____

 _____

 _____

 _____

_____

 _____

2.

 _____

 _____

 _____

3.

_____

_____

_____

 _____

 _____

 _____

4.

Level 2

ORGANIZE INFORMATION: Sequence of Events

Extension: Ask children to draw three pictures that show something that happened. The pictures should be in sequence.

4

Is It Yours?

Write the words to show who owns something.
Remember to add **'s.**

1. Jenna   sock

_____
- - - - - - - - - - - - - - - - - -
_____

2. Tom   dog

_____
- - - - - - - - - - - - - - - - - -
_____

3. Coco   apple

_____
- - - - - - - - - - - - - - - - - -
_____

4. Grandma   house

_____
- - - - - - - - - - - - - - - - - -
_____

5. Maria   cat

_____
- - - - - - - - - - - - - - - - - -
_____

78

Extension: Ask children to write other possessive phrases, using classmates' names.

Level 2
STRUCTURAL CLUES: Possessives

5

Macmillan/McGraw-Hill

Name: _____   Date: _____

COCO CAN'T WAIT!

Write the word that completes each sentence.

1. Coco wants to see _____.

   Mom   Grandma   Dad

2. Grandma lives on the _____.

   roof   hill   mountain

3. Coco goes to Grandma's _____.

   house   tree   roof

4. Grandma is not _____.

   away   there   old

5. Coco and Grandma will meet under the _____.

   house   basket   tree

Extension: Ask children to write a sentence telling about their favorite part of the story. They may also want to illustrate the sentence.

Name: _____   Date: _____

COCO CAN'T WAIT!

Circle the picture that goes with each sentence.

| with | one | very | much | here | no |

1. Grandma will go with us in the car.

2. Coco has a very big dog and a much smaller cat.

3. Grandma's shirt has no dots and no flowers.

4. Pam has one brother and one sister.

5. Put the flowers here on the table.

Extension: Have children write sentences about things they like to do with a grandparent or another adult.

Macmillan/McGraw-Hill

COCO CAN'T WAIT!

Write a word from the box to complete each sentence.

with	one	very	much	here	no

_____

- - - - - - - - - - -

1. I saw a _____ little cat in the yard.

_____

- - - - - - - - - -

2. The apples are _____ the bananas.

_____

- - - - - - - - - -

3. There is not _____ milk in the glass.

_____

- - - - - - - - - -

4. Put the toys _____ in the basket.

_____

- - - - - - - - - -

5. Are there _____ or two books on the desk?

Macmillan/McGraw-Hill

5
Level 2
High-Utility Words

Extension: Invite children to choose a word from the box, write a sentence using it, and draw a picture to go with the sentence.

81

Name: _____

Date: _____

Coco Can't Wait!
VOCABULARY:
HIGH-UTILITY WORDS

PUZZLE FUN

Write a word from the box to complete each sentence.

| with | one | very | much | here | no |

_____

1. I play _____ Coco and Sammy.

2. How _____ will that doll cost ?

3. She can jump _____ high.

4. He ate all but _____ of the apples.

5. There are _____ turtles _____ .

Find the six words you wrote above. Circle them.

```
M U C H A Z C N O
E W V E R Y H P S
C U G F O N E K M
H E R E Z W I T H
```

Extension: Invite children to choose one or more of the sentences and draw pictures for them.

Macmillan/McGraw-Hill

FILL WORDS

Write the letters **ill** to make words. Then use each word to complete a sentence.

1. f_____   2. s_____   3. w_____

4. h_____   5. b_____

6. The bird has a large _____.

7. I _____ put the food on the tray.

8. My cat sits on the _____ of the window.

9. No trees grow on the _____.

10. She wants to _____ the basket with apples.

Level 2
Short Vowels and Phonograms /i/ -ill

Extension: Challenge children to write as many words as they can that end with the letters **ill**.

Macmillan/McGraw-Hill

Name: _____ Date: _____

Grape Words, Truck Words

Say the name of each picture. Circle the letters that stand for the beginning sound.

1. gr   tr

2. gr   tr
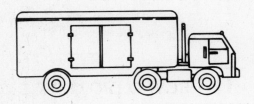

3. gr   tr

4. gr   tr

5. gr   tr

6. gr   tr
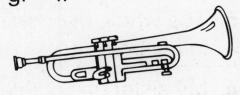

7. gr   tr
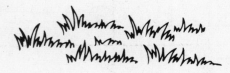

8. gr   tr
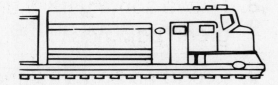

9. gr   tr

10. gr   tr

84   **Extension:** Challenge children to write one sentence with a **gr** word and one with a **tr** word.

Level 2
Consonant Blends /gr/ *gr*, /tr/ *tr*   10

Macmillan/McGraw-Hill

REAL OR MAKE-BELIEVE?

Put a ✔ under **Real** if the sentence tells about something that could really happen. Put a ✔ under **Make-Believe** if the sentence tells about something that couldn't really happen.

	Real	Make-Believe
1. I saw a pig dance a jig.		
2. We ate some watermelon.		
3. My mother went down to the bay.		
4. I put my pet dragon in the doghouse.		
5. The whale did not fit in my bathtub.		
6. My sister has a little toy bear.		
7. A fly was on my pie.		
8. I have some yellow and green pajamas.		
9. Grandma has a talking llama in her yard.		
10. A wheel fell off my wagon.		

Macmillan/McGraw-Hill

10
Level 2
Fantasy and Reality

Extension: Have children write some other sentences to add to the list. Classmates can tell whether the sentences tell about real or make-believe things.

FINISH IT!

Underline the words that belong in each sentence.

1. One (pig   pigs) has two (wig   wigs).

2. The (dragon   dragons) play with a (wagon   wagons).

3. Some (goat   goats) sail in (boat   boats).

4. A big (whale   whales) swims with two (pail   pails).

5. A (bear   bears) wears two (bow   bows) in its hair.

Extension: Ask children to rewrite some of the sentences so that different words are singular and plural.

Level 2
STRUCTURAL CLUES: Plurals

10

Down by the Bay
PHONICS: Short Vowels
and Phonograms /i/ -id

Name: _____ Date: _____

Lid Words

Write the letters **id** to complete the word. Then do what each sentence tells you to do.

_____
- - - - - - - -
1. Find the l_____. Color it red.

_____
- - - - - - -
2. Find the one that h_____.
Color it green.

_____
- - - - - - -
3. Find the k_____. Color it brown.

_____
- - - - - - - -
4. Find what someone d_____ with paint.
Color it yellow.

_____
- - - - - - -
5. Find the place where you get r_____ of things.
Color it blue.

Level 2
Short Vowels and Phonograms /i/ -id

Extension: Invite children to choose one of the pictures and write a short story about it.

87

WHAT'S THE STORY?

Number the pictures **1, 2,** or **3** to show the order in which things take place in the story.

1. Maria put on a clean shirt. She got on her bike and went to see Tom. Tom and Maria made a birdhouse.

_____ _____ _____
- - - - - - - - - - - - - - - - - - - - -
_____ _____ _____

2. The mother bird made a nest in the tree. She laid three eggs. When the baby birds came, she fed them.

_____ _____ _____
- - - - - - - - - - - - - - - - - - - - -
_____ _____ _____

Extension: Ask children to draw three pictures showing something that happened in 1-2-3 order. Then they can write sentences about their sequence of events.

Level 2
ORGANIZE INFORMATION: Sequence of Events
2

Macmillan/McGraw-Hill

Name: _____   Date: _____

DOWN BY THE BAY

Draw a line from the picture to the words that tell what the animal had or did in the story.

I.    with a polka dot tail

2.    rowing a boat

3.    kissing a goose

4.    wearing a wig

5.    pulling a wagon

Macmillan/McGraw-Hill

DOWN BY THE BAY

Write the word from the box that completes each sentence.

down	by	Where	grow	go	Do

_____
- - - - - - - - - - -

1. The watermelon plant will _____ fast.

_____
- - - - - - - - - -

2. We ran _____ to the bay.

_____
- - - - - - - - - -

3. _____ is the moose?

_____
- - - - - - - - - -

4. _____ you see the llama in pajamas?

_____
- - - - - - - - - -

5. A goat sat _____ the goose.

_____
- - - - - - - - - -

6. I can't _____ home.

Extension: Have children write or tell a story, beginning with one of the sentences.

Level 2
High-Utility Words

6

Macmillan/McGraw-Hill

Name: _____ Date: _____

DOWN BY THE BAY

Underline the sentence that tells about the picture.

down	by	where	grow	go	do

1. Where did the whales go?

The whales like to go for a swim.

2. The baby will grow fast.

The baby is by the goose.

3. The cat ran up the stairs.

The cat ran down the stairs.

4. The goose will go with the moose.

The goose jumped down.

5. The bear will do a dance.

The bear will do the dishes.

5

Level 2
High-Utility Words

Extension: Invite children to choose a word from the box, write a
sentence using the word, and draw a picture to go with the sentence.

FUN WITH WORDS

Write the word from the box that completes each sentence. Circle the picture that goes with the sentence.

| down | by | Where | grow | go | do |

_____

‒ ‒ ‒ ‒ ‒ ‒ ‒ ‒ ‒ ‒ ‒

1. The bear sat _____ by the goat.

_____

‒ ‒ ‒ ‒ ‒ ‒ ‒ ‒ ‒ ‒ ‒

2. The flower didn't _____ well.

_____

‒ ‒ ‒ ‒ ‒ ‒ ‒ ‒ ‒ ‒ ‒

3. _____ did my cat go?

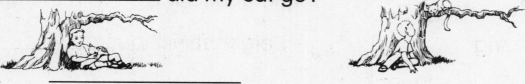

_____

‒ ‒ ‒ ‒ ‒ ‒ ‒ ‒ ‒ ‒ ‒

4. We will _____ in the car.

Extension: Direct children to choose a sentence and a picture and write two more sentences to go with them.

Macmillan/McGraw-Hill

Down by the Bay
PHONICS: SHORT VOWELS
AND PHONOGRAMS /i/ -ig

Name: _____   Date: _____

PIG WORDS

Circle the word that goes with the picture. Write the word on the line.

1.   _____

wig   big   one _____ pig

2.   _____

jig   fig   a pig dancing a _____

3.    _____

big   wig   a pig in a _____

4.   _____

rig   dig   a pig that will _____

5.    _____

rig   wig   a pig in a _____

5   Level 2
Short Vowels and Phonograms /i/ -ig

Extension: Challenge children to choose one of the phrases and add a
second line to make a two-line rhyme.

93

Name: _____ Date: _____

Down by the Bay
PHONICS: CONSONANT
BLENDS /dr/ *dr*

DRESS WORDS

Circle the word that tells about each picture.

1. drop
   dress
   drag

2. draw
   drop
   drill

3. drum
   drive
   draw

4. dry
   drive
   droop

5. dream
   dress
   dragon

6. drapes
   drill
   drum

Extension: Direct children to write **dr** on a sheet of paper and then to write as many words as they can think of that begin with those letters.

Level 2
Consonant Blends /dr/ *dr*
6

Macmillan/McGraw-Hill

WRITE RIGHT

Write the word that completes each sentence. Use the pictures to help you.

mow   mowed
_____

- - - - - - - - - - - - - - - - - -

1. The bear will _____.

_____

- - - - - - - - - - - - - - - - - -

2. The bear _____.

plant   planted
_____

- - - - - - - - - - - - - - - - - -

3. The cat_____ a bean.

_____

- - - - - - - - - - - - - - - - - -

4. Will he _____ again?

_____

- - - - - - - - - - - - - - - - - -

5. He _____ many beans.

5 Level 2
Inflectional Endings -ed

Extension: Let pairs of children list action words and then add **-ed** to them.

95

CAN YOU TELL THE STORY?

I The plants needed water.

2 Jasper sprayed water on the plants.

3 The plants are much better now.

Number the sentences **1, 2, 3** so that they tell the story.
A story has a beginning, a middle, and an end.

I. ____ Jack jumped down the beanstalk.

____ A giant was at the top.

____ Jack climbed the beanstalk.

2. ____ Then we watered the plant.

____ We put the bean in the ground.

____ We found a bean.

Extension: Ask children to write three sentences on strips of paper that tell a story. Have them exchange their stories with a classmate who puts the sentences in order.

ORGANIZE INFORMATION: Sequence of Events

Level 2

6

Macmillan/McGraw-Hill

Name: _____   Date: _____

HILL WORDS

Look at the picture. Choose the word that
completes each sentence. <u>Write the word.</u>

1. Jill can _____ it.

    mill   fill   gill

2. Dad will pay the _____.

    sill   till   bill

3. We had fun on the _____.

    hill   dill   fill

4. Dad likes to cook on the _____.

    spill   chill   grill

5. The cat _____ look for a mouse.

    hill   will   bill

5   Level 2
Short Vowels and Phonograms /i/ -ill

Extension: Invite children to choose a sentence, use it to begin a story,
and continue the story.

97

Macmillan/McGraw-Hill

JASPER'S BEANSTALK

Circle **Yes** or **No** to tell what Jasper did.

1. Yes   No   Jasper found a bean.

2. Yes   No   He ate the bean.

3. Yes   No   He planted the bean.

4. Yes   No   Jasper watered it.

5. Yes   No   He picked beans.

6. Yes   No   He waited for the beanstalk
to grow.

7. Yes   No   He dug up the bean.

8. Yes   No   Jasper looked for giants.

9. Yes   No   He climbed the beanstalk.

10. Yes   No   Jasper saw a giant.

Macmillan/McGraw-Hill

98   **Extension:** Invite children to write their own questions about the story.
Classmates can answer the questions.   Level 2
Story Comprehension   10

Name: _____ Date: _____

JASPER'S BEANSTALK

Write the words from the box to complete each sentence.

He	When	again	that	long	all

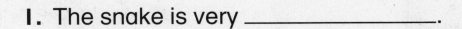

1. The snake is very _____.

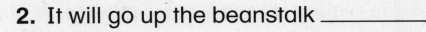

2. It will go up the beanstalk _____.

3. The water is _____ gone.

4. _____ will we get there?

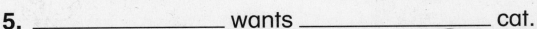

5. _____ wants _____ cat.

6

Level 2
High-Utility Words

Extension: Invite children to choose several words from the box and write sentences for them.

Name: _____   Date: _____

JASPER'S BEANSTALK

Look for the word from the box that is in each
sentence. Write the word.

He	When	again	that	long	all

1. He will mow the grass.

_____

- - - - - - - - - - - - - -

_____

2. The cat has a long tail.

_____

- - - - - - - - - - - - - -

_____

3. When will the bus come?

_____

- - - - - - - - - - - - - -

_____

4. They all fit in the basket!

_____

- - - - - - - - - - - - - -

_____

5. What is in that box?

_____

- - - - - - - - - - - - - -

_____

Extension: Direct children to write sentences, leaving a blank for a
missing word in each. Classmates can write the missing words.

Level 2
High-Utility Words

5

Macmillan/McGraw-Hill

WHAT'S THE ANSWER?

Write the words from the box to complete the questions. Circle the picture that answers each question.

he	When	again	that	long	all

_____

I. Which one has a _____ nose?

_____

2. Who has _____ the bananas?

_____

3. _____ do you go in the water?

4. What will _____ have to do

_____?

5. What can _____ baby do?

HUG WORDS

Write the letters **ug** to complete the word. Draw a line from the question to the picture that answers the question.

1. Who can give you a h _____?

2. What can you put into a m _____?

3. What might eat a b _____?

4. What has a pl _____?

5. What might chew on a r _____?

Extension: Suggest that children write a question and draw pictures for other **-ug** words. Classmates can circle the correct picture.

Level 2
Short Vowels and Phonograms /u/ -ug

5

Macmillan/McGraw-Hill

Slide Words, Plant Words

Say each picture name. Circle the letters that stand for the beginning sound.

1.

pl

sl

2.

pl

sl

3.

pl

sl

4.

pl

sl

5.

pl

sl

6.

pl

sl

7.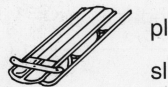

pl

sl

8.

pl

sl

8 Level 2
Consonant Blends /sl/ *sl*, /pl/ *pl*

Extension: Invite children to choose three pictures and write sentences for them.

CUMULATIVE VOCABULARY REVIEW

Look at the words in the box. Underline the word
your teacher says.

1. are away am	**2.** across blue clean	**3.** can run bad
4. no it by	**5.** where why what	**6.** all he one
7. very when white	**8.** that over much	**9.** from here long
10. play said down	**11.** grow jump going	**12.** walk with under

Macmillan/McGraw-Hill

CUMULATIVE VOCABULARY REVIEW

Circle the word or words that tell about the picture.

1.

run with it

clean with it

2.

go away

come in

3.

very little

very long

4.

go up

go down

5.

grow

walk

6.

clean

jump

CUMULATIVE VOCABULARY REVIEW

Circle the word that goes in the blank.

1. can _____

go

by

2. are _____

do

clean

3. very _____

with

much

4. _____ here

down

long

5. _____ again

when

do

6. _____ big

when

grow

Name: _____   Date: _____

CUMULATIVE VOCABULARY REVIEW

Underline the words that tell about the picture.
Write the words on the lines.

1.  clean it   help it grow

_____

- - - - - - - - - - - - - - - -

_____

2.  are long   are clean

_____

- - - - - - - - - - - - - - - -

_____

3.  runs away   ·   grows again

_____

- - - - - - - - - - - - - - - -

_____

4.  that cat   down here

_____

- - - - - - - - - - - - - - - -

_____

ADD -*S* WORDS

Write the word that completes the sentence.

_____
- - - - - - -
1. The teacher _____ to the class.

     talk   talks

_____
- - - - - - -
2. Uncle Lou _____ the plants.

     water   waters

_____
- - - - - - -
3. The man _____ the door.

     lock   locks

_____
- - - - - - -
4. The cat _____ up the tree.

     climb   climbs

_____
- - - - - - -
5. Maria _____ her dog.

     walk   walks

Extension: Encourage children to use each word they wrote in a
sentence of their own.

Level 3
Inflectional Endings -*s*

5

Macmillan/McGraw-Hill

WHAT HAPPENED?

Look at each picture. Draw a line from the picture to the sentence that tells what happened.

1.    The floor got wet.

2.    The paint spilled on the rug.

3.    The girl lost her book.

4. 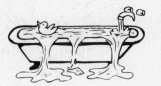   Penny fell on the floor.

5.    Luis was late for school.

5

Level 3
Cause and Effect

Extension: Have children talk about what was the cause and what was the effect in each situation.

GRASSHOPPER WORDS

Draw a line from the grasshopper to the other pictures that begin with the same sound as **grasshopper.**

Extension: Have children draw a picture that includes things whose names begin with the same sound as **grasshopper.**

Level 3
Consonant Blends /gr/ *gr*

5

Macmillan/McGraw-Hill

TWINS

Read the story and look at the pictures. Then answer the questions.

Scott and Sara are twins.
They were born on the same day.
They have the same mother and father.
They live in the same house.
Scott likes to play ball. Sara likes to swim.

1. Tell how Scott and Sara are alike.

_____

_____

_____

_____

2. Tell how Scott and Sara are different.

_____

_____

_____

_____

Extension: Have children suggest other ways in which Scott and Sara could be alike and different.

NUT WORDS

Draw a line from each picture to the sentence that tells about it.

1.

The squirrel has a nut.

2.

Mother will cut the cake.

3.

Carlos will shut the window.

4.

The car is stuck in a rut.

5.

They paint the hut.

Extension: Have children underline the words that end with the letters ut in the sentences.

Level 3
Short Vowels and Phonograms /u/ -ut
5

Macmillan/McGraw-Hill

CHANGES

Draw a line from the picture to the picture and sentence that tell how things change.

1.

We can make a tower with blocks.

2.

Day turns into night.

3.

The boy got bigger.

4.

A chick comes from an egg.

5.

Some seeds become flowers.

5 | Level 3
Story Comprehension

Extension: Have children draw a picture of something and then draw another picture showing how it changed.

AN EGG IS AN EGG

Circle the word that completes each sentence.
Then write the word.

1. We _____ wear seat belts in the car.

   always   never

2. We _____ get into a car with a stranger.

   always   never

3. We _____ wash our hands before we eat.

   always   never

4. We _____ look both ways when we cross the street.

   always   never

5. We _____ play with matches.

   always   never

114   **Extension:** Help children write their own always/never sentences.

Level 3
High-Utility Words

5

Macmillan/McGraw-Hill

AN EGG IS AN EGG

Write the word from the box that completes each sentence.

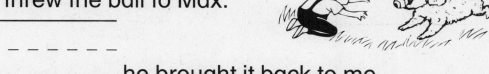

Some	Then

1. Puff had four kittens.

_____

_____ were black.

2. I threw the ball to Max.

_____

_____ he brought it back to me.

3. Many animals live in the zoo.

_____

_____ have four legs.

4. Put your coat on.

_____

_____ go outside.

5. We are planting flowers.

_____

_____ are big.

Name: _____ Date: _____

AN EGG IS AN EGG

Circle the word that completes each sentence.

we	many

1. I see (many   we) balloons.

2. Can (many   we) wash the car?

3. There are (many   we) birds in the tree.

4. Shall (many   we) play ball today?

5. The bug has (many   we) legs.

116
Extension: Have children create sentences using the words **many** and **we**.

Level 3
High-Utility Words
5

Macmillan/McGraw-Hill

SCRAMBLED WORDS

Unscramble the mixed-up letters to make a word
that ends with the letters **ick.** Write the word.

1. See the cat **ickl** her kitten. _____

2. Put the **ickst** in the fire. _____

3. Adam does a funny **icktr**. _____

4. The little pig made a **ickbr** house. _____

5. Mother will **ickp** a yellow flower. _____

Macmillan/McGraw-Hill

MAKE A CH WORD

Write the letters **ch** to finish each picture name.

1. The _____ ick lives in the barn.

2. Grandma sat on the _____ air by the window.

3. We played a game of _____ eckers.

4. The _____ imney is made of bricks.

5. She ate a ham and _____ eese sandwich.

Extension: Have children look for magazine pictures of things whose names begin with the same sound as cheese.

Level 3
Consonant Digraphs /ch/ *ch*
5

Macmillan/McGraw-Hill

START WITH ST WORDS

Circle the word that names the picture.

 **I.**   star   stump   sack

  2.   stove   stamp   owl

 **3.**   pan   stem   stove

 **4.**   stick   stamp   shoe

 **5.**   sand   stool   stove

5   Level 3
Consonant Blends /st/ *st*

Extension: Have children look in books and magazines for pictures of
things whose names begin with the same sound as star.

119

CAMPING FUN

Read the story.

Dad made a big fire.

Jim helped put up the tent.

Ann cooked a hot dog.

They had fun camping.

Does the sentence tell the main idea of the story?
Write **yes** or **no**.   _____

1. Dad made a big fire.   _____

2. They had fun camping.   _____

3. Ann cooked a hot dog.   _____

4. Jim helped put up the tent.   _____

5. Write the sentence that tells the main idea.

_____

_____

_____

Extension: Show a picture from a magazine or book, and have children
write a sentence that tells the main idea of the picture.

Level 3
Main Idea and Supporting Details

5

Macmillan/McGraw-Hill

RIDDLE PICKS

Read each riddle. Circle the answer. Then write the
word on the line.

1. I can be used to make a house.
I am hard.   _____

brick   boot   sick   I am a _____ .

2. You do this with your foot.
You do it to a ball.   _____

trick   clean   kick   You _____ a ball.

3. I come from a tree.
I can be used to make a fire.   _____

tick   stick   cow   I am a _____ .

4. I am a sound a clock makes.
If you listen, you will hear me.   _____

sick   bell   tick   I say _____ -tock.

4

Level 3
Short Vowels and Phonograms /i/ -ick   **Extension:** Have children circle the words that end with the letters ick.   **121**

A DAY IN THE PARK

Add **ed** to the word to make a new word that completes each sentence.

_____
- - - - - - -

1. The girl walk _____ her dog.

_____
- - - - - - -

2. Ned and Joe play _____ ball.

_____
- - - - - - -

3. Wendy jump _____ over the puddle.

_____
- - - - - - -

4. Rob look _____ at the roses.

_____
- - - - - - -

5. Kelly dump _____ the sand out of the pail.

122   **Extension:** Have children use each -ed word in another sentence.

Level 3
Inflectional Endings -ed   5

Macmillan/McGraw-Hill

GROUP IT

Fill in the circle next to each word that belongs in the group.

1. Colors

○red   ○duck   ○blue   ○white

2. People

○mother   ○sister   ○father   ○cat

3. School

○sun   ○desk   ○book   ○pen

4. Parts of the Body

○arm   ○hat   ○leg   ○nose

5. Numbers

○two   ○one   ○bat   ○three

5   Level 3
Categories

Extension: Have children name other things that belong in each category.

123

WHOSE BABY?

Draw a line from each baby to its father and
mother.

1.

2.

3.

4.

5.

Extension: Have children draw a picture of another animal and its
parents.

Level 3
Story Comprehension

5

WHOSE BABY?

Circle the word that completes each sentence. Then write the word.

_____

- - - - - - - - -

1. is   on   This _____ Boots.

2. this   is   Boots likes to play with _____.

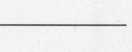

_____

- - - - - - - - -

3. whose   is   This _____ Fred.

_____

- - - - - - - - -

4. is   this   Fred runs on _____ wheel.

_____

- - - - - - - - -

5. Whose   This   _____ house is this?

Level 3
High-Utility Words

Extension: Have children write words that describe Boots and Fred.

125

Macmillan/McGraw-Hill

WHOSE BABY?

mother	father	baby

Use a word from the box to answer each question.

1. Who runs in the park?

_____

_ _ _ _ _ _ _ _ _ _

_____

2. Who plays with the baby?

_____

_ _ _ _ _ _ _ _ _ _

_____

3. Who is little?

_____

_ _ _ _ _ _ _ _ _ _

_____

4. Who has a black hat?

_____

_ _ _ _ _ _ _ _ _ _

_____

5. Who has a ball?

_____

_ _ _ _ _ _ _ _ _ _

Extension: Have children draw pictures of things they might see in a park. Help them label the things they draw.

WHOSE BABY?

mother	father	baby	is	whose	this

Choose the word from the box that completes each sentence.

1. I help my _____ plant flowers.

2. Is _____ your new truck?

3. A turtle _____ an animal with a shell.

4. The _____ likes to play.

5. My _____ likes to read.

6. I don't know _____ coat this is.

FIT A WORD

Write the letters **it** to complete the words in the sentences.

1. We went on a trip in the car.

_____

- - - - - - -

     I did not want to s _____ by Ben.

_____

- - - - - - -

2. Ben can't f _____ in the car.

     He is too big!

_____

- - - - - - -

3. Mary b _____ into a peach.

_____

- - - - - - -

4. The peach had a p _____.

     Mary lost her tooth!

5. Mark is strong.

_____

- - - - - - -

     He h _____ the ball over the fence.

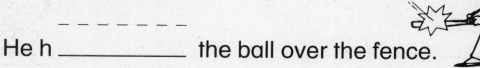

Extension: Have children pantomime the actions of each sentence as you read it aloud.

Level 3
Short Vowels and Phonograms /i/ -it

5

Macmillan/McGraw-Hill

What's The Word?

Circle the pictures whose names begin with the same sound as **white.** Then write a word from the box beside each **wh** picture.

whale whistle whip wheel whisper

1. _____

2. _____

3. _____

4. _____

5. _____

6. _____

7. _____

8. _____

Macmillan/McGraw-Hill

8

Level 3
Consonant Digraphs /hw/wh

Extension: Have children cut out magazine pictures of objects or actions whose names begin with the same sound as **white.**

129

BE A HIT WITH -IT WORDS

Circle the word that completes the sentence.

1. Tina _____ the ball.

   sit   hit   fit

2. He can _____ on the chair.

   sit   pit   hit

3. Darla won't _____ on the stool.

   fit   pit   hit

4. Pete _____ the apple.

   fit   bit   sit

5. The peach has a _____ in it.

   fit   pit   bit

130 **Extension:** Have children make up new sentences for three of the **-it** words they circled.

Level 3
Short Vowels and Phonograms /i/-it   5

Macmillan/McGraw-Hill

Name: _____   Date: _____

GRANDMA'S BIRTHDAY

Write the word from the box that completes each sentence.

eat	eats	leave	leaves	sit	sits

1. Grandma _____ cake.

2. We _____ cake, too.

3. Grandma _____ at the table.

4. We _____ at the table, too.

5. Uncle George _____ Grandma's house.

6. We _____ Grandma's house, too.

6

Level 3
Inflectional Endings -s

Extension: Have children use the -s words in their own sentences.

131

Macmillan/McGraw-Hill

Name: _____ Date: _____

TRAP A WORD

Circle the letters that stand for the beginning sound
in the name of each picture.

1.

tr   gr

2.

tr   gr

3.

tr   gr

4.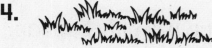

tr   gr

5.

tr   gr

6.

tr   gr

7.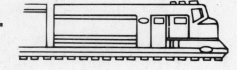

tr   gr

8.

tr   gr

132

Extension: Have children cut out magazine pictures of things whose
names begin with the same sound as truck or grapes. Then let children
share their pictures with the class.

Level 3
Consonant Blends /tr/ *tr*, /gr/ *gr*

8

WHAT WILL HAPPEN?

Look at each picture. Then underline the sentence that tells what will happen.

1. The man will drop the tray.

The man will eat the food.

2. Lynn will need her umbrella.

Lynn will play outside.

3. Aunt Jane will bake a cake.

Aunt Jane won't have the things she needs.

4. Lee will trip and fall.

Lee will win the race.

Level 3
ORGANIZE INFORMATION: Cause and Effect

4

Extension: Have children identify the cause and the effect in each situation.

133

Macmillan/McGraw-Hill

ANIMALS, ANIMALS, ANIMALS

Read each story. Fill in the circle by the title that
tells the main idea of the story.

1. Parrots can talk.

They climb ladders.

They ring bells.

They are colorful.

○ Parrots Are Fun

○ Big Birds

2. Tigers have striped fur.

They hunt other animals.

They roar.

People like to visit them at the zoo.

○ All About Tigers

○ A Day at the Zoo

Extension: Have children give the main idea for a book they are
reading.

ORGANIZE INFORMATION: **Main Idea
and Supporting Details**

Level 3

2

Macmillan/McGraw-Hill

EVERYTHING GROWS

Reread the story. Circle the pictures of the things that can grow.

1.

2.

3.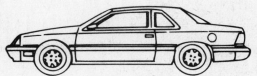

4.

5.

6.

7.

8.

9.

10.

EVERYTHING GROWS

sisters	brothers	goes

Read the story. Choose the word from the box that completes each sentence.

Lisa and her family go to the beach.
Lisa has two sisters.
They play with a ball.
Lisa has three brothers.
They sit on the sand.
Lisa goes in the water with her mother and father.

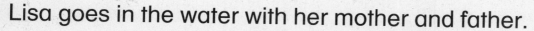

1. The _____ sit on the sand.

2. Lisa _____ in the water.

3. The _____ play with a ball.

4. Lisa has two _____.

5. Lisa has three _____.

Macmillan/McGraw-Hill

EVERYTHING GROWS

Read the story. Circle the word that completes each sentence.

This is Wise Old Owl.

He lives in the forest.

He knows about plants and animals.

He sees in the dark.

He goes to many places in the forest.

1. Wise Old Owl _____ in the forest.

   lives   sings   knows

2. Wise Old Owl _____ about plants and animals.

   looks   makes   knows

3. Wise Old Owl _____ to many places in the forest.

   sees   from   goes

4. Wise Old Owl _____ in the dark.

   walks   sees   goes

4 Level 3
High-Utility Words

Extension: Have children draw pictures of things that Wise Old Owl sees in the forest.

137

Macmillan/McGraw-Hill

Name: _____   Date: _____

EVERYTHING GROWS

everything	sisters	goes	knows	brothers

Find and circle each word from the box in the puzzle. Then write the words you found.

t o k b j k l s m h
e v e r y t h i n g
n v c o h w q s f g
u b c t h g p t y u
p l k h e w s e r y
b g o e s h n r t a
v x z r f h n s e t
p y g s k n o w s d

1. _____   2. _____   3. _____

4. _____   5. _____

138   Extension: Have children use each word in a sentence.

Level 3
High-Utility Words   10

RHYMING WORDS

Circle each picture whose name rhymes with **made**.

1.

2.

3.

4.

5.

6.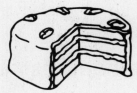

7.

8.

FILL IN THE RIGHT WORD

| brother | bricks | broom | bridge | bright |

Write the word from the box that completes each sentence.

1. I use a _____ to sweep the floor.

2. Carlos is my oldest _____.

3. The candle has a _____ flame.

4. The house is made of _____.

5. The _____ goes over the river.

140

Extension: Have children think of other words that begin with the same sound as branch.

Level 3
Consonant Blends /br/ *br*
5

Macmillan/McGraw-Hill

BED WORDS

Write the letter or letters to make a word that tells about the picture.

1. _____ed

2. _____ed

3. _____ed

4. _____ed

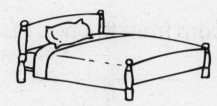

5. _____ed

6. _____ed

Macmillan/McGraw-Hill

6
Level 3
Short Vowels and Phonograms /e/ -ed

Extension: Have children use each word that ends with the letters **ed** in a sentence.

141

CUTTING TOOLS

Use the chart to show how a scissors and a knife are alike and different. Put a check in the box next to the words that tell about each one.

	scissors	knife
one blade		
cuts food		
two blades		
sharp		
made of steel		
cuts paper		

Extension: Have children name other things that can be cut with a pair of scissors or a knife.

Level 3
ORGANIZE INFORMATION:
Comparison and Contrast

8

Macmillan/McGraw-Hill

WHAT HAPPENS?

Look at the picture. Underline the sentence that tells what will happen.

1.

   He rides on a pony.

   He goes inside the house.

2.

   She fixes the tire.

   She rides to school.

3.

   She goes outside.

   She goes to bed.

4.

   The rain comes in.

   The sun comes out.

5.

   The tree has no leaves.

   The tree has many leaves.

5 Level 3
ORGANIZE INFORMATION: Cause and Effect

Extension: Have children identify the cause and the effect in each situation.

143

Name: _____ Date: _____

BROOM WORDS

Write the letters **br** under the pictures whose names begin with the same sound as **broom.**

1.

2.

3.

4.

5.

144

Level 3
Consonant Blends /br/ br

5

Macmillan/McGraw-Hill

WHITE RABBIT'S COLOR BOOK

Circle the sentences that tell what happened in the story.

1. White Rabbit finds a box of crayons.

2. White Rabbit jumps into the tub of paint.

3. White Rabbit goes for a walk.

4. White Rabbit turns orange.

5. White Rabbit washes.

6. White Rabbit turns red, then purple.

7. There is no more water.

8. White Rabbit turns brown.

8 | Level 3
Story Comprehension

Extension: Have children draw pictures of things that are the same color as White Rabbit after one of her color changes.

145

Name: _____ Date: _____

WHITE RABBIT'S COLOR BOOK

Together	make

Write the words from the box to complete the sentences.

_____ _____
- - - - - - - - - - - - - -

1. _____, you and I _____ we.

_____ _____
- - - - - - - - - - - - - -

2. _____, many branches _____ a tree.

_____ _____
- - - - - - - - - - - - - -

3. _____, two eyes _____ you see.

Extension: Have children write their own sentences with **together** and **make,** using the sentence pattern from this page.

Level 3
High-Utility Words

6

Macmillan/McGraw-Hill

WHITE RABBIT'S COLOR BOOK

Look	warm	How

Underline the words from the box that you see in the story.

Look at the snow!

How should Bob dress?

Will Bob be warm?

Color the things that Bob can wear to be warm.

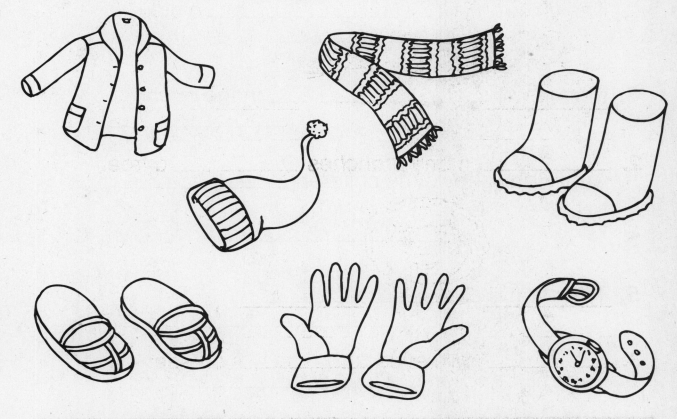

Macmillan/McGraw-Hill

8 Level 3
   High-Utility Words

Extension: Have children draw a picture of a winter activity and label it.

147

Name: _____   Date: _____

WHITE RABBIT'S COLOR BOOK

| about   warm   make   look   how   together |

Look at the pictures. Write the word from the box that completes each sentence.

1. The book tells _____ making a pie.

2. The children will _____ a pie.

3. Marvin will _____ in the oven.

4. Aunt Patty shows the children _____ to make a pie.

5. The oven is _____.

6. The children work _____.

Extension: Have children write three sentences about something they made.

Name: _____ Date: _____

TICK-TACK-TOE

In each group of words, find the word that rhymes
with **cake**. Circle the word and write it on the lines.

bat	shake	is
make	boat	look
shoe	we	lake

1. _____

2. _____

3. _____

hut	broom	snake
bridge	rake	whip
bake	hit	chain

4. _____

5. _____

6. _____

Macmillan/McGraw-Hill

6   Level 3
Long Vowels and Phonograms /ā/ -ake

Extension: Have children choose a word that ends with the letters **ake**,
then write a sentence and draw a picture to go with it.

149

MR. WIND BLOWS!

Help Mr. Wind blow the **bl** words back to the correct pictures. Draw lines from the **bl** words to the pictures the words name.

blocks

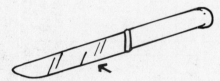

blade

blanket

blimp

blink

black

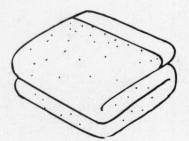

Macmillan/McGraw-Hill

150

Extension: Have children make up sentences using two of the bl words.

Level 3
Consonant Blends /bl/ *bl*

6

Cumulative Vocabulary Review

Look at the words in the box. Underline the word your teacher says.

1. again about under	**2.** whose here how	**3.** goes good grow
4. when from some	**5.** look long clean	**6.** with this then
7. where warm one	**8.** make much walk	**9.** down knows do
10. not found never	**11.** always away all	**12.** he we no
13. many very my	**14.** by it is	**15.** mother father brothers

CUMULATIVE VOCABULARY REVIEW

Circle the word that tells about the picture.

1.

sisters

brothers

2.

goes

look

3.

make

about

4.

baby

mother

5.

many

how

6.

whose

we

CUMULATIVE VOCABULARY REVIEW

Circle the word that goes in the blank.

1. _____ dog

whose

many

2. three _____

about

brothers

3. a _____ coat

together

warm

4. _____ of the books

some

then

5. a book _____ trains

about

this

6. _____ on time

knows

always

7. a little _____

how

baby

8. _____ for a walk

knows

goes

CUMULATIVE VOCABULARY REVIEW

Underline the words that tell about the picture.
Write the words on the lines.

1. run together   play together

_____

- - - - - - - - - - - - - - - -

_____

2. everything green   everything under

_____

- - - - - - - - - - - - - - - -

_____

3. we jump   I jump

_____

- - - - - - - - - - - - - - - -

_____

4. about father   about baby

_____

- - - - - - - - - - - - - - - -

_____

WHAT HATTIE SEES

Write the word from the box that completes each sentence.

| eyes   legs   tail   nose   ears   body |

1. First Hattie sees a _____ in the bushes.

2. Then she sees two _____.

3. Next Hattie sees two _____.

4. Then she sees two _____.

5. Then Hattie sees a _____.

6. Finally, she sees a _____,

   and she knows it's a fox!

6

Level 4/Unit 1
Selection Vocabulary

Extension: Have children find a picture of a cat or dog and name its parts using the selection vocabulary.

155

Macmillan/McGraw-Hill

Name: _____ Date: _____

Hattie and the Fox
PHONICS: CONSONANT
BLENDS /bl/ *bl*

BLOCK WORDS

Write the letters **bl** to finish each word. Circle the picture the word names.

I. _____ ock

2. _____ ack

3. _____ ouse

4. _____ anket

5. _____ ossom

Extension: Have children write a sentence to go with each picture they circled.

Level 4
Consonant Blends /bl/ *bl*

5

Name: _____ Date: _____

Hattie and the Fox
PHONICS: SHORT VOWELS
AND PHONOGRAMS /i/ -ig

BIG WORDS

Write the word from the box that completes each sentence.

big	dig	pig	wig	rig

1. I am not big.

I am a baby _____.

2. I ate like a pig.

I got very _____.

3. This will look silly on a fig.

It is a _____.

4. This can't dance a jig.

It is a big _____.

5. Do you need a hole that's big?

Use this to _____.

5 Level 4
Short Vowels and Phonograms /i/ -ig

Extension: Ask children to write pairs of rhyming -ig words, such as big/pig. They can then write sentences for each pair of words.

157

WHAT ARE THEY LIKE?

Put a ✔ under the picture if the word tells about the animal.

1. smart				
2. watchful				
3. clever				
4. sly				
5. afraid				

Extension: Ask children to choose a character from a story they know, draw a picture of the character, and write three words that tell about the character.

Level 4/Unit 1
ANALYZE STORY ELEMENTS: Character

5

Macmillan/McGraw-Hill

WHY DID IT HAPPEN?

Look at each picture. It shows what happened.
Underline the sentence that tells why it happened.

Effect	**Cause**

1.

Grandma lives near us.

Grandma lives far away.

Grandma came to see us.

2.

Dad rides the bike.

Dad will go away.

Dad needs some help.

3.

They are looking for a cat.

The girl wants a new ball.

Mother wants a green hat.

4.

The dog wants the bone.

The dog will go away.

The dog hit its nose.

WHAT WILL HAPPEN NEXT?

Draw a line from each pair of sentences to the
picture that shows what will happen next.

1. The fox is in a hurry to get
   down the hill.

   What will the fox do?

2. The fox puts too much
   food in a bag.

   What will the fox have to do?

3. The fox wants to get something
   for the horse to eat.

   What will the fox get?

4. The fox is hot.

   What will the fox do?

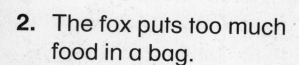

 Extension: Invite pairs of children to create oral sentences that answer
the questions.

Macmillan/McGraw-Hill

Level 4/Unit 1
Make, Confirm, or Revise Predictions

4

FIGURE IT OUT!

Circle the picture that answers the question.

1. Tina wants some apples.

Where will she go?

2. Ken went to the pond.

What did he do?

3. Kim would like a bat.

Where will she go?

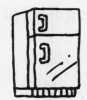 

4. Lee has five cents.

What can he get?

5. Jasper had a birthday party.

What did he do?

Macmillan/McGraw-Hill

5 Level 4/UNIT 1
Draw Conclusions

Extension: Ask children to draw another picture that could also answer each question.

161

PICTURE THE STORY

Read the story. Number the pictures to show the order in which Hattie went to see her friends.

Hattie had a very busy day. First, she jumped rope with Goose.

Next, she went to see Horse. Horse was outside picking apples. Hattie helped Horse pick a big basket of apples. Then, they ate and ate.

Next, Hattie went to see Pig. Pig had a new basketball. They played and played.

Then, Hattie saw Fox. He read a story to her.

When Hattie got home, she was happy. "That was a fun day," she said.

_____   _____   _____   _____

Extension: Have children make up sentences to tell what Hattie and each friend did.

Level 4/Unit 1
ORGANIZE INFORMATION: Sequence of Events
4

Macmillan/McGraw-Hill

Name: _____   Date: _____

HATTIE AND THE FOX

Show who said the words. Write the number of the picture on the line next to the words.

1.    _____ "It's a fox! It's a fox!"

2.   _____ "MOO!"

3.   _____ "Who cares?"

4.    _____ "So what?"

5.    _____ "Well, well!"

6.    _____ "Good grief!"

6

Level 4/Unit 1
Story Comprehension

Extension: Invite children to write another sentence that each animal might have said.

163

Macmillan/McGraw-Hill

Hattie and the Fox
PHONICS: LONG VOWELS
AND PHONOGRAMS /ī/ -ime

Name: _____ Date: _____

TIME WORDS

Look at the picture. Write the word that completes
the sentence.

  Use this to tell the _____.

            lime   time

2.  What can you get with a _____?

            dime   mime

3.  There is _____ on the pants.

            prime   grime

4. Use a _____ to make juice.

            lime   dime

5.  Taking money is a _____.

            prime   crime

164   **Extension:** Invite children to write other sentences for three of the **-ime** words.

Macmillan/McGraw-Hill

Name: _____ Date: _____

Hattie and the Fox
PHONICS: Consonant
Blends /fl/ *fl*

FLUTE WORDS

Underline and write the word that names the picture.

1. flame
   flute

   _____

2. flood
   flashlight

   _____

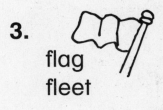

3. flag
   fleet

   _____

4. flow
   fly

   _____

5. flowers
   floors

   _____

6. flea
   flat

   _____

7. floor
   flute

   _____

8. flavor
   flame

   _____

Macmillan/McGraw-Hill

8 Level 4/Unit 1
   Consonant Blends /fl/ *fl*

Extension: Have children write sentences for five of the words they wrote.

165

FILL IT IN

Underline and write the word to complete each sentence.

| kind | any | nice | trouble | gave | animals |

1. What _____ of dog do you want?

    any   kind   gave

2. Mother _____ me a pony.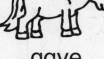

    nice   animals   gave

3. How many _____ do you have?

    trouble   nice   animals

4. A dog can be _____.

    kind   trouble   gave

166 **Extension:** Have children write questions using the words from the box.

Level 4
Selection Vocabulary
4

Macmillan/McGraw-Hill

Name: _____ Date: _____

GUESS WHAT HAPPENS

Put a ✔ on the picture that answers the question.

1. Ken calls the dog to go for a walk.

What will the dog do?

2. The mouse sees the cheese.

What will the mouse do?

3. Jan wants to go for a ride.

What animal will she get on?

4. Ned wants to help.

What will he do?

Macmillan/McGraw-Hill

---

4 | Level 4
Make, Confirm, or Revise Predictions

Extension: Have children draw a picture showing something that is about to happen. Classmates can tell what will happen next.

Name: _____ Date: _____

TREE WORDS

Circle the word that names the picture.

1.
trip
tray
trick

2.
trap
trail
tree

3.
truck
tray
triangle

4.
try
trunk
tractor

5.
trip
trailer
tree

6.
tray
trumpet
treat

7.
trash
treasure
trail

8.
trip
trash
trick

Extension: Challenge children to write sentences with words that begin with tr.

Level 4
Consonant Blends /tr/ *tr*

8

Macmillan/McGraw-Hill

PICTURE CLUES

Draw lines from the pictures to the words that name what the people do.

1.    drummer

2.    pet shop owner

3.    doctor

4.    police officer

5.    teacher

6.    firefighter

7.    carpenter

8.    farmer

Macmillan/McGraw-Hill

8 | Level 4
Use Illustrations

Extension: Ask children to draw a picture showing what they would like to be. Then have them label their picture.

Name: _____ Date: _____

HOT WORDS

Circle the letter or letters that stand for the sound you hear at the beginning of each picture name. Write the letter or letters.

1. h   t

_____ ot

2. r   t

_____ ot

3. d   c

_____ ot

4. p   g

_____ ot

5. cl   sp

_____ ot

6. kn   sl

_____ ot

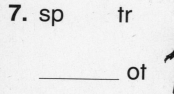

7. sp   tr

_____ ot

8. d   r

_____ ot

Macmillan/McGraw-Hill

LOOKING AND THINKING

Look at the picture. Underline the sentence that tells about the picture.

1.

Dan gave Ken a cat.

Ken likes all animals.

He can come out.

2.

Kim has a pony.

Nan likes to jump.

They like each other.

3.

Ben knows how to help.

Ben found a baby.

The baby is very small.

4.

Sam likes animals.

Sam can read.

Sam is in trouble.

Macmillan/McGraw-Hill

4 Level 4
Make Inferences

Extension: Ask children to draw a picture that gives clues about something they like to do. Classmates can use the picture to guess what that activity is.

Name: _____   Date: _____

ANY KIND OF DOG

Read the questions. Write the number of the question in the box under the picture that answers the question.

1. Who wants any kind of dog?

2. Who said a dog was too much trouble?

3. Who gave a mouse and a lion?

4. Who got a lamb and a pony?

5. Who got a dog?

6. Who gave a dog?

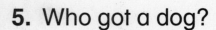

Extension: Ask children to write a sentence telling about their favorite part of the story. They could also illustrate the sentence.

Level 4
Story Comprehension
6

Macmillan/McGraw-Hill

MICE WORDS

Help the mice get to the cheese. Circle all the words that rhyme with **mice.** Draw a line to connect the words.

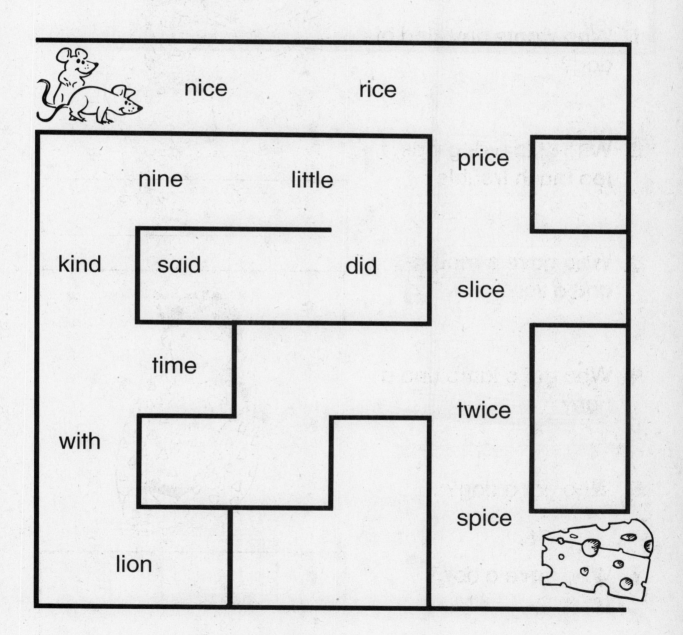

nice   rice

price

nine   little

kind   said   did   slice

time

twice

with

spice

lion

6

Level 4
Long Vowels and Phonograms /ī/ **-ice**

Extension: Challenge children to write sentences for three of the words they circled.

173

Macmillan/McGraw-Hill

SHOE WORDS

Write the word from the box that names each picture.

shelf	sheep	shirt	shave
shell	shoe	ship	shop

1.

_____

2.

_____

3.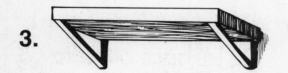

_____

4.

_____

5.

_____

6.

_____

7.

_____

8.

_____

Extension: Challenge children to write as many words as they can that begin with the letters **sh**.

Level 4
Consonant Digraphs /sh/ sh

8

Macmillan/McGraw-Hill

WHAT'S THE WORD?

Write the word from the box that completes each sentence.

morning	beautiful	pond	silly	called	count

1. Pig likes to get up early in the _____.

2. Pig sees himself in the _____.

3. The animals _____ each other to come and look.

4. Sheep thinks he looks _____.

5. The animals feel _____ after they jump into the pond.

6. The animals laugh because Frog can't _____.

6 Level 4/Unit 1
Selection Vocabulary

Extension: Have children give oral sentences using the vocabulary words.

175

Macmillan/McGraw-Hill

UP, DOWN, ALL AROUND

Circle the picture that the sentence tells about.

I. The hen is on the log.

2. The rabbit is next to the rabbit hole.

3. The frog is under the water.

4. The goat is across from the sheep.

5. The mouse ran down the tree.

Extension: Invite children to write sentences that tell where an animal is. They can also draw pictures about the sentences.

Level 4/Unit 1
ORGANIZE INFORMATION:
Spatial Relationships

5

WHAT WOULD THEY SEE?

Read the sentences. Draw a line to the picture that answers each question.

1. Pig went to Hen's house. What might Pig see there?

2. Rabbit will give Goat something to eat. What will Goat get?

3. Frog wants Sheep to see where Frog likes to sit. What will Sheep see?

4. Sheep wants Goat to see what Sheep will make from wool. What might Goat see?

5. Mouse wants Pig to see what gives Mouse trouble. What might Pig see?

Macmillan/McGraw-Hill

5

Level 4
Make, Confirm, or Revise Predictions

Extension: Ask children to write a riddle similar to the ones on the page. Classmates can draw a picture that answers the riddle.

177

JET WORDS

Write the words to make each sentence tell about the picture.

1.

We will _____ on the _____.

     let   get   net   jet

2.

Will you _____ me hold your _____?

     let   set   bet   pet

3.

I _____ the frog is _____.

   met bet   vet wet

4.

The _____ is on the TV _____.

   vet net   jet set

178

Extension: Challenge children to choose one of the sentences and add another sentence that tells more about what is happening.

Level 4/Unit 1
Short Vowels and Phonograms /e/ -et

4

Macmillan/McGraw-Hill

Name: _____   Date: _____

She Words

Write the letters **sh** under each picture whose name begins with the same sound as **she.**

1.
_____

2.
_____

3.
_____

4.
_____

5.
_____

6.
_____

7.
_____

8.
_____

9.
_____

10.
_____

11.
_____

12.
_____

12
Level 4
Consonant Blends /sh/ *sh*

Extension: Challenge children to choose three **sh** words and write a tongue twister by using all three words in a sentence.

Name: _____   Date: _____

NUMBER PICTURES

Read each story. Number the pictures to show the order of things in the story.

1. Four silly animals jumped into the pond. First, Frog hopped in. Rabbit jumped in next. Then Hen went into the water. Mouse was the last and made a little splash.

_____   _____   _____   _____

2. Some animals went for a ride in a car. Goat got in first. Sheep went next. Then came Frog. Last, Hen jumped in. They drove to the pond.

_____   _____   _____   _____

3. The animals had a party at the pond. Hen came first with some corn. Mouse came next with cheese. Pig came with apples. Then Rabbit came with carrots.

_____   _____   _____   _____

Extension: Invite children to write their own story about the animals and draw pictures for classmates to number in sequence.

Level 4
Sequence of Events

12

Macmillan/McGraw-Hill

GET THE PICTURE?

Circle the picture that shows what each person needs.

1.

2.

3.

4.

5.

Macmillan/McGraw-Hill

⬛ 5

Level 4/Unit 1
ORGANIZE INFORMATION: Use Illustrations

Extension: Invite children to write sentences for several of the picture pairs. For example, *A hat would help the farmer feel better.*

181

SEVEN SILLIES

Write the names of the animals to complete the story.

Sheep   Pig   Goat   Rabbit   Hen   Mouse

One morning _____ looked into the

pond and saw a handsome animal. He called over

to _____, who saw a beautiful animal, and

he called over to _____, who saw a

gorgeous animal. That animal called to the splendid

_____, who wanted _____ to

come and look. She called to dear, little

_____. Then they all jumped into the

water. Frog laughed at them. He said they were

seven sillies. But there were really only six.

182   **Extension:** Invite children to continue the story by telling what happened after the animals laughed at Frog's mistake.

Level 4
Story Comprehension   6

SLEEP WORDS

Underline the word that completes the sentence.
Write the word.

1. He wants to go to _____.

    keep   sleep   beep

2. The water is _____.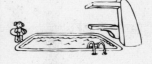

    sweep   sheep   deep

3. She wants to _____ the frog.

    weep   keep   sweep

4. The hill is very _____.

    steep   sleep   peep

5. He likes to _____.

    jeep   deep   sweep

Macmillan/McGraw-Hill

5

Level 4
Long Vowels and Phonograms /ē/ -eep

Extension: Ask children to choose one of the sentences and write another sentence to go with it.

183

SCRUB WORDS

Add the parts together to make a word. Write the word. Circle the picture that goes with the word.

1. scr + ub = _____

2. scr + een = _____

 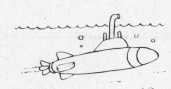

3. scr + ew = _____

4. scr + atch = _____

5. scr + eech = _____

Extension: Have children choose one of the pictures and write a sentence to go with it.

Macmillan/McGraw-Hill

MATCH-UPS

Find the word that completes each sentence. Write the letter of the answer on the line.

| king head woods along food fallen |

_____ 1. Come __ with me to
see Grandmother.   **a.** king

_____ 2. We went for a walk
in the ____.   **b.** fallen

_____ 3. Let's go tell the ____
about the dragon.   **c.** woods

_____ 4. What did he put on
his ____?   **d.** along

_____ 5. I need to get some
____ for my alligator.   **e.** food

_____ 6. Has the log ____ into
the pond?   **f.** head

6 Level 4
Selection Vocabulary

Extension: Encourage children to write other sentences or a story using the words in the box.

185

Name: _____ Date: _____

WHAT'S THE EFFECT?

Read the sentences. Then circle the picture that shows what happened.

1. Gina is climbing a tall tree.

She falls to the ground.

2. The baby is eating.

She drops her spoon.

3. It is very dark.

Henry can't see inside the tent.

4. Dad is cooking dinner.

He goes to answer the phone.

5. Last night it snowed.

Ann wants to go out.

Extension: Ask children to choose one of the pictures they circled and write a sentence that tells the effect.

Level 4/Unit 1
ORGANIZE INFORMATION: Cause and Effect

5

Macmillan/McGraw-Hill

WORKING WITH AN ENDING

Add **ing** to each word. Write the new word. Then write the **ing** word that completes each sentence.

1. fall _____

_____

2. look _____

_____

3. jump _____

_____

4. wash _____

_____

5. They are _____ rope.

6. Is the sky _____?

7. I like _____ at flowers.

8. My cat is _____ its paws.

8   Level 4/Unit 1
STRUCTURAL CLUES: Inflectional
Endings *-ing*

Extension: Invite children to choose a sentence, use it to begin a story, and then continue the story.

187

Name: _____   Date: _____

CHICKEN WORDS

Color each picture whose name begins with the same sound as **chicken.**

Extension: Ask children to look in magazines and books for words that begin with the same sound as **chicken.**

Level 4/Unit 1
Consonant Blends /ch/ ch   15

Macmillan/McGraw-Hill

STORY PARTS

Read the story. Write your answers.

The king called the animals together in a cave in the woods. There was trouble. The king needed help to get food. He wanted to be sure the animals had plenty of food for the winter. All the animals helped bring food to the cave. They had good food all winter long.

1. Who is the story about?

_____

2. Where does the story take place?

_____

3. What does the king want?

_____

_____

4. What do the animals do after the meeting?

_____

Macmillan/McGraw-Hill

4 Level 4
Character, Plot, Setting

Extension: Invite children to write a story about what the animals might do when the spring comes.

189

Name: _____ Date: _____

CAKE WORDS

Read the sentences. Do what they tell you to do.

1. Take **b** away from **bake.**
   Put in **c.**

   Write the new word.

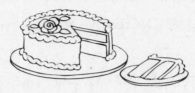

_____

2. Take **f** away from **fake.**
   Put in **r.**

   Write the new word.

_____

3. Take **m** away from **make.**
   Put in **l.**

   Write the new word.

_____

4. Take **qu** away from **quake.**
   Put in **sn.**

   Write the new word.

_____

5. Take **br** away from **brake.**
   Put in **fl.**

   Write the new word.

_____

Extension: Invite children to write another riddle for a word that ends
with the letters **ake**. Classmates can write the answer to the riddle.

Level 4
Long Vowels and Phonograms /ā/ -ake

5

Macmillan/McGraw-Hill

ORDER IN A STORY

Read each story. Number the pictures **1, 2, 3** to show the order in which things happened.

1. First, Pam read a book.

Next, she played with her cat.

Then, she went for a ride on her bike.

_____   _____   _____

2. Dad and Len went in the car to the woods.

They put up a tent.

Then, they went fishing.

_____   _____   _____

Level 4/Unit 1
ORGANIZE INFORMATION: Sequence of Events
2

Extension: Ask children to write three sentences that tell the order in which they did something.

IT'S MINE!

Read each sentence. Circle the word that completes the sentence. Then write the word.

1. Have you seen the _____ cat?
   kings   king's

2. The _____ lost their pet cat.
   boys   boy's

3. The _____ bone is in the hole.
   dogs   dog's

4. _____ skate has lost a wheel.
   Nans   Nan's

5. Those two _____ have brown fur.
   bears   bear's

6. Is the _____ tail long?
   cows   cow's

Extension: Have children write possessive phrases using a friend's name and the name of something that belongs to the friend. For example, *Maria's pencil.*

Level 4/Unit 1
STRUCTURAL CLUES: Possessives   6

Macmillan/McGraw-Hill

THE STORY OF CHICKEN LICKEN

Look at each picture. First, write the letter of the character's name. Then, number the order in which the characters met Chicken Licken. Use the story if you need help.

a. Cock Lock   **b.** Drake Lake   **c.** Gander Lander

d. Goose Loose   **e.** Henny Penny   **f.** Duck Luck

		Who Is It?	**When Did They Meet?**
1.		_____	_____
2.		_____	_____
3.		_____	_____
4.		_____	_____
5.		_____	_____
6.		_____	_____

12 Level 4/Unit 1
Story Comprehension

Extension: Let children choose two story characters and write a short story about them.

193

CRY WORDS

Write the word from the box that completes each sentence

try	fly	sky	cry	dry

1. Why did the baby _____?

2. Let's go _____ our kites.

3. Use this to _____ the dog.

4. Snow fell from the _____.

5. She will _____ to fix the bike.

Extension: Invite children to choose a sentence and write another sentence that tells what happened next.

Name: _____   Date: _____

Sk Words

Read the word in each row. Then circle the picture whose name has the same beginning sound.

1. skin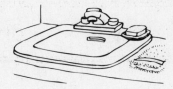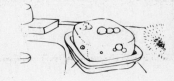

2. skip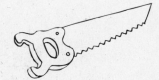

3. sky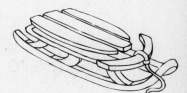

4. skillet

5. skid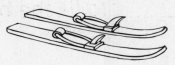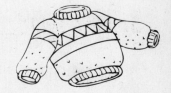

5

Level 4/Unit 1
Consonant Blends /sk/ *sk*

Extension: Invite children to write other words that begin with the same sound as **skirt**.

195

CAN YOU DO IT?

Read and follow each set of directions.

1. Put an X on something that can fly. Circle something that can run.

2. Draw a tail on the mouse. Put some cheese in front of the mouse.

3. Put a hat on the clown. Draw a little dog next to the clown.

4. Put a box around the thing that you might find in the woods. Put a line over the thing that has a head.

Extension: Invite children to write other sets of directions for class-mates to follow.

Level 4/Unit 1
STUDY SKILLS: Follow Directions 8

Macmillan/McGraw-Hill

Unit Vocabulary Review

Look at the words in the box. Underline the word
your teacher says.

1. nice eyes ears	**2.** nose never whose	**3.** trouble together tail
4. is ears goes	**5.** head how food	**6.** king kind knows
7. any animals always	**8.** count about pond	**9.** along always about
10. many mother morning	**11.** body baby brothers	**12.** fallen called along
13. never nice this	**14.** woods warm we	**15.** silly some sisters

ONE MONDAY MORNING

cook	queen	prince	visit	return	knight

Read each sentence. Underline the word that goes in the blank. Write the word.

1. The _____ called on the boy.   visit

   prince

2. The _____ got on the pony.   return

   knight

3. Who came to _____ you?   visit

   return

4. When will the king _____?   prince

   return

5. The _____ made good food.   cook

   visit

6. That _____ has a big crown.   queen

   cook

Extension: Invite children to write a story using as many words from the box as possible. They may draw a picture to go with the story as well.

Macmillan/McGraw-Hill

Name: _____ Date: _____

WHAT IS THE CAUSE?

Read the question. Look at the picture. Underline
the answer.

Effect	**Cause**

1. Why did the milk spill?

The cup was too full.
The knight bumped the cup.
The cup was too tall.

2. Why did the queen
go away?

No one was home.
The king said to go away.
The prince was late.

3. Why did the queen
call the knight?

He tells good stories.
She wants the dragon
to go away.
The king is missing.

4. Why did the cook
run in?

He saw a mouse.
The food was not cooked.
The pot was running over.

Level 4/Unit 2
**ORGANIZE INFORMATION: Cause and
Effect**

4

Extension: Have children choose one of the effects and tell a partner
what happens next.

199

CUT WORDS

Look at the picture. Choose the word that
completes the sentence and tells about the picture.

I. The prince has a _____ on his hand. cut
nut

2. Who lives in this _____? rut
hut

3. The door is _____. shut
cut

4. The animal will eat the _____. but
nut

5. I want to skate, _____ I can't. but
rut

200 **Extension:** Have children choose several words that were not used.
Then ask them to draw pictures and write sentences for the words.

Level 4
Short Vowels and Phonograms /u/ -ut 5

Macmillan/McGraw-Hill

Name: _____   Date: _____

WHAT'S NEXT?

Look at the picture. Draw what could happen next.

1.

2.

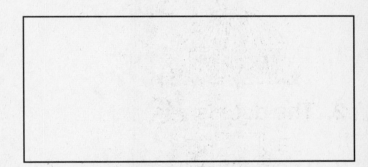

3.

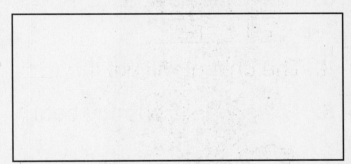

4.

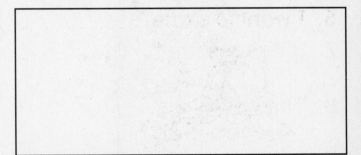

4

Level 4/Unit 2
Make, Confirm, or Revise Predictions

Extension: Invite children to draw a picture that classmates can use as a springboard for making a prediction. Classmates can write or draw their predictions.

GUESS WHAT I GOT!

Look at the picture of the gift. Read each sentence.
Circle **Yes** if the sentence helps you know what is
inside. Circle **No** if it will not.

1. The gift is not heavy.		Yes	No
2. The paper is green.		Yes	No
3. The gift feels soft.		Yes	No
4. The gift has a bow.		Yes	No
5. The shape is a teddy bear.		Yes	No
6. The ribbon is red.		Yes	No
7. Birthdays are fun.		Yes	No
8. The bow is big.		Yes	No

Extension: Challenge children to think of a gift they would like to give
someone. Ask them to write three clues about it. Classmates can guess
the gift.

202

Level 4/Unit 2
Make Inferences

8

WHAT IS REAL?

Read each sentence. Put an **X** under **Real** if the sentence tells something that could really happen. Put an **X** under **Make-believe** if the sentence tells something that could not really happen.

Real   **Make-believe**

I. The cook made a big cake.

2. A prince got a yellow cat.

3. The alligator talked to the boy.

4. The goose sang a song.

5. The king wore a crown.

6. A cat rode a horse with wings.

7. A knight called to the dragon.

8. The barber cut the bug's hair.

9. The guard watched for danger.

10. A tailor sewed some pants.

Macmillan/McGraw-Hill

Level 4/Unit 2
Fantasy and Reality

Extension: Invite children to write three more sentences, some of which could really happen and some of which could not. Classmates can tell which is which.

Name: _____ Date: _____

DRAGON WORDS

Color the picture if its name begins with the same sound as **dry**.

1.

2.

3.

4.

5.

6.

7.

8.

9.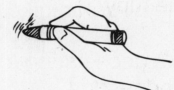

10.

11.

12.

Extension: Challenge children to make a list of words beginning with **dr** and then to write sentences for some of the words.

Level 4
Consonant Blends /dr/ dr   12

Macmillan/McGraw-Hill

WHO CAME TO VISIT?

Many came to see the boy. Choose the letters beside the names of the visitors and write them next to the day or days they came.

a. king   b. guard   c. little prince   d. barber

e. jester   f. queen   g. cook   h. knight

1. Monday   ____ ____ ____

2. Tuesday   ____ ____ ____ ____

3. Wednesday   ____ ____ ____ ____ ____

4. Thursday   ____ ____ ____ ____ ____ ____

5. Friday   ____ ____ ____ ____ ____ ____ ____

6. Saturday   ____ ____ ____ ____ ____

____ ____ ____

6 Level 4/Unit 2
Story Comprehension

Extension: Invite children to tell a partner a story about what happened when everyone finally got together with the boy.   **205**

GAME WORDS

Read the sentence. Write the word that completes each sentence.

1. The lion is not _____.

shame   same   tame

2. The king has wealth and _____.

game   fame   came

3. Put the picture into a _____.

flame   frame   dame

4. Let's play this _____.

dame   game   same

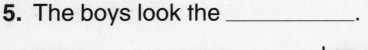

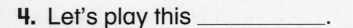
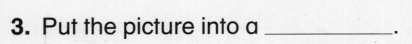

5. The boys look the _____.

same   came   lame

Macmillan/McGraw-Hill

206 **Extension:** Suggest that children try writing two-line rhymes using words that end in **ame**.

Level 4/Unit 2
Long Vowels and Phonograms /ā/ -ame

5

Prize Words

Look at the picture. Write the word that completes each sentence.

1. You have to _____ to play this well.

practice   prize

2. Is the _____ for me?

pretty   present

3. Use this to _____ your pants.

press   print

4. The flower is very _____.

pretty   prune

5. What is the _____ of the car?

present   price

5

Level 4/Unit 2
Consonant Blends /pr/ *pr*

Extension: Challenge pairs of children to write other sentences for the words they did not use in the sentences.

207

YOU'LL SOON GROW INTO THEM, TITCH

brother   sister   pants   pair   socks   clothes

Circle the word that completes the sentence. Write the word.

1. I called my _____.   sister   clothes

2. Sam is her _____.   pants   brother

3. I have red _____.   sister   socks

4. My _____ are clean.   pair   clothes

5. Where are my _____?   sister   pants

6. This is an old _____ of shoes.   pair   shoes

Extension: Direct children to draw a picture of themselves, including what they are wearing that day. Have them label the various articles of clothing.

Macmillan/McGraw-Hill

WHAT SHOULD THEY DO?

Look at the pictures. Read the sentences. Then write your answers to the question.

1.  Dad is hungry.
What will he do?

_____

_____

2.  It is raining outside.
What can I do inside?

_____

_____

3.  Mother heard the baby cry.
What will she do?

_____

_____

4.  The socks have holes in them.
What would you do?

_____

_____

Macmillan/McGraw-Hill

4 Level 4/Unit 2
ORGANIZE INFORMATION: Problem and Solution

Extension: Have children pose other problems to a classmate. The classmate could offer solutions to the problems.

209

BIG PIG WORDS

Look at the picture. Circle the word that goes with it. Write it on the line.

1.    dig or rig   _____

2.    wig or fig   _____

3.    jig or pig   _____

4.    fig or big   _____

5. 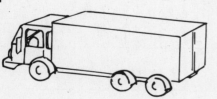   rig or dig   _____

Extension: Ask children to choose three of the words they wrote and use them in a single sentence. The sentence can be a silly one.

Level 4

Short Vowels and Phonograms /i/ -ig

5

Macmillan/McGraw-Hill

Name: _____   Date: _____

You'll Soon Grow into
Them, Titch
PHONICS: Consonant Blends /st/ *st*

STACK THE WORDS

Complete the words below by writing **st**. Then draw
a line to the picture that goes with each word.

1. _____ ar

2. _____ airs

3. _____ ack

4. _____ ain

5. _____ ool

6. _____ ump

7. _____ amp

8. _____ ove

Macmillan/McGraw-Hill

Extension: Have children draw other pictures whose names begin with
the same sound as **stop**. Classmates can guess the name of each
child's picture.

NUMBER THEM, PLEASE

Read each story. Number the pictures to show the right order.

1. First, Matt washed an apple. Then, Mom cut it into four pieces for him. Matt ate all but one piece. He gave it to his sister.

_____   _____   _____   _____

2. My sister dressed her doll. First, she put the dress on her. Next, a hat went on. Then, she put on the doll's sweater. Last, she took off the hat and put on socks.

_____   _____   _____   _____

Extension: Challenge children to draw a four-picture story, cut out each picture, and ask a classmate to put the pictures in the right sequence.

Level 4/Unit 2
ORGANIZE INFORMATION: Sequence of Events

2

Macmillan/McGraw-Hill

MAKE IT SHORT

Read each story. Write one sentence to tell what
the story is about.

1.

Tim and Jim were friends. Tim liked Jim's new
sweater. Jim liked Tim's new sweater. Each boy put
on the other boy's sweater.

_____

2.

Three baby birds were in the nest. It was time to
fly. First, one baby bird tried to fly. Then the other
two tried to fly. They had fun flying.

_____

_____

Macmillan/McGraw-Hill

2 Level 4
Summarize

Extension: Let partners take turns telling stories. Each partner could
give a short summary of the other's story.

Picture Clues

Underline the sentence that tells about the picture.

 **1.** It was time to put out the light.

The boy will play in the park.

 **2.** She needs to go out and play.

The sweater is too big.

 **3.** Mother Bird will get some food.

The babies will fly away.

 **4.** Mother likes to make pants.

Mother has almost finished a sock.

 **5.** The cat wants milk.

The cat wants to get down.

Extension: Invite children to look at the pictures in storybooks and tell the class what information the pictures give them.

CLEAN CLOTHES WORDS

Make the word. Circle the picture that goes with the word.

1. cl + ip = _____

2. cl + ock = _____

3. cl + aw = _____

4. cl + oud = _____

5. cl + own = _____

6. cl + ay = _____

7. cl + ap = _____

8. cl + ub = _____

8   Level 4
Consonant Blends /kl/ *cl*

Extension: Invite children to write tongue twisters using several of the **cl** words they wrote.

215

Macmillan/McGraw-Hill

STORY PARTS

Read the story. Write the answer to each question.

Pam and her dad sat by the pond. They were fishing. Then Dad's hat fell into the pond. How could they get it out? Pam said they should use the fishing rod. So Dad used his rod to catch his hat.

I. Where does the story take place?

_____

2. Who is the story about?

_____

3. What is the problem?

_____

4. How is the problem solved?

_____

_____

Extension: Ask children to choose a story they know, tell where it takes place, tell who is in it, and describe what happens.

Level 4/Unit 2
ANALIZE STORY ELEMENTS:
Character, Plot, Setting

4

Macmillan/McGraw-Hill

YOU CAN HAVE MINE

Read the sentence. Circle the picture that shows
what each person gave.

1.    You can have my ___.

2.    You can have my ___.

3.    You can have our ___.

4.    The new baby can
have my ___.

Extension: Invite children to write some suggestions as to what the
children can do with the clothes they have outgrown.

217

-OLD WORDS

Read the sentence and look at the picture. Write the word that completes the sentence.

1. Tim wants to _____ a kitten.

mold   hold   fold

2. The day is very _____.

told   sold   cold

3. Mother has a ring of _____.

gold   told   bold

4. The big house was _____.

told   sold   bold

5. There is _____ on the old bread.

mold   cold   sold

218

Extension: Challenge children to write pairs of rhyming sentences that end with **-old** words.

Level 4
Long Vowels and Phonograms /ō/ -old

5

Macmillan/McGraw-Hill

SWELL SWEATER WORDS

Read each question. Circle the picture whose name begins with the same sound as **swell** and answers the question.

1. What do you put on when you are cold?

2. What could you play on in a park?

  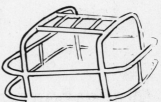

3. Which is a beautiful bird that swims?

4. What can you use to turn off lights?

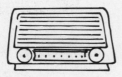 

5. What can you do in the water?

5 Level 4/Unit 2
Consonant Blends /sw/ *sw*

Extension: Have children choose a question and its picture answer and write a story about it.

Seven Blind Mice

great strange agree elephant whole turn

Write the letter next to the word that completes the
sentence.

a. strange   **b.** elephant   **c.** turn
d. great   **e.** agree   **f.** whole

1. _____ When is it my _____?

2. _____ An _____ is a big animal.

3. _____ I do not _____ with you.

4. _____ What is that _____ noise?

5. _____ We had a _____ time.

6. _____ Who ate the _____ pie?

Find the words from the box above and circle them.

7. agreebnrturn

8. sbwholeckfd

9. celephantdhs

10. greatstrange

Extension: Invite children to make their own word search puzzle, using
six words of their own choosing.

Level 4/Unit 2
Selection Vocabulary

12

Macmillan/McGraw-Hill

NICE WORDS

Read the sentence. Then look at the picture. Write the word that completes the sentence.

twice	nice	rice	mice	slice

1. Put jam on a _____ of bread.

2. The boy has _____ as many

   dogs as the girl.

3. Some _____ ran up the clock.

4. A sweater feels _____

   on a cold day.

5. I like to eat _____.

Macmillan/McGraw-Hill

Extension: Invite children to choose one of the words and write their own sentence for it, leaving a blank where the word should go. Classmates can then exchange sentences to write the missing word.

GET THE PICTURE?

Circle the picture that shows what each person needs.

1.

2.

3.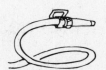

4.

5.

Extension: Challenge children to think of a person who has a particular job. Have them name one or two things the person would need to do the job.

Level 4
ORGANIZE INFORMATION:
Use Illustrations

5

Macmillan/McGraw-Hill

Name: _____ Date: _____

MAKE A GUESS

Circle the picture that shows what each person felt
while playing a game.

1. John put his hand in the bag.

   He felt something that was

   sharp at one end and soft at

   the other end. What did he feel?

2. Jan could feel something soft.

   It had two arms and two legs.

   What did she feel?

3. Sam could feel something

   round and smooth.

   What did he feel?

4. Pat could feel something hard.

   The thing had four wheels.

   What did she feel?

4 | Level 4/Unit 2
Make, Confirm, or Revise Predictions

Extension: Invite children to draw pictures that classmates can use to
make further predictions. Classmates can write or draw their
predictions.

Name: _____ Date: _____

TELL THE STORY

Number the pictures to show the order in which the story took place. Write one sentence for each picture to tell the story.

_____

_____

_____

_____

1. _____

_____

2. _____

_____

3. _____

_____

4. _____

Level 4/Unit 2
ORGANIZE INFORMATION: Sequence of Events
8

Macmillan/McGraw-Hill

WHOLE WHEEL WORDS

Color each picture whose name begins with the same sound as **white.**

1.

2.

3.

4.

5.

6.

7.

8.

9.

10.

11.

12.

12 | Level 4/Unit 2
Consonant Digraphs /hw/ *wh*

Extension: Give children the words **why, what, where,** and **when,** and ask them to write questions using the words.

225

WHERE IS IT?

Look at the picture. Then, underline the word or words that complete each sentence.

1. The doll is ___ the kite.

    over   under

2. The elephant is ___ the tiger and the bear.

    above   next to

3. The bear is ___ the tiger.

    next to   under

4. The kite is ___ of everything.

    at the bottom   in the middle

5. The kite is ___ the doll.

    beneath   on top of

Macmillan/McGraw-Hill

Extension: Allow partners to make a list of words that show the position of things in the classroom. Suggest that they write sentences for some of the words.

Level 4/Unit 2
ORGANIZE INFORMATION: Spatial
Relationships

5

END IT

Underline the word that completes the sentence.

1. Red Mouse thought the leg was a ____.

pillar   log

2. Green Mouse thought the trunk was a ____.

worm   snake

3. Yellow Mouse thought the tusk was a ____.

pin   spear

4. Purple Mouse thought the top of the head was a ____.

cliff   mountain

5. Orange Mouse thought the ear was a ____.

paper   fan

6. Blue Mouse thought the tail was a ____.

string   rope

7. White Mouse thought the strange thing was an ____.

ant   elephant

8. White Mouse was ____.

right   wrong

8 Level 4/Unit 2
Story Comprehension

Extension: Challenge children to draw a picture showing something the elephant and the seven mice might have done together.

227

SLIDE WORDS

Take a trip down the slide. Circle each word that rhymes with **slide.**

START

1. hide

2. told

3. ride

4. wide

5. red

6. slid

7. side

8. hid

9. child

10. tide

11. bride

12. stride

Extension: Suggest that children try writing two-line rhymes using words that end in **ide.**

Level 4/Unit 2
Long Vowels and Phonograms /ī/ -ide

12

Macmillan/McGraw-Hill

THINK, THANK, THIN WORDS

Change the first letter of each word to **th.** Write the word that tells about each picture.

corn

pin

1.

_____

2.

_____

numb

pink

3.

_____

4.

_____

bird

nimble

5.

_____

6.

_____

6

Level 4/Unit 2
Consonant Digraphs /th/ *th*

Extension: Challenge pairs of children to write sentences for several of the **th** words on this page.

229

Name: _____ Date: _____

WHERE CAN YOU FIND IT?

Look at the Table of Contents page. Read the
questions and write your answers.

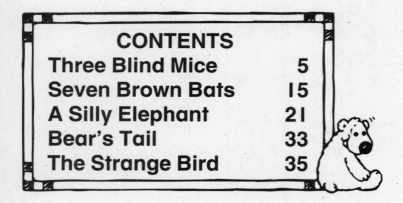

CONTENTS

Three Blind Mice	5
Seven Brown Bats	15
A Silly Elephant	21
Bear's Tail	33
The Strange Bird	35

1. How many stories are there in the book?

_____

2. On what page does "Three Blind Mice" begin?

_____

3. What story begins on page 21?

_____

4. On what page does a story about bats begin?_____

5. Is the bear story near the front or the back of the
book?

_____

Extension: Challenge children to write two more questions about the
Table of Contents. Classmates can answer the questions.

Macmillan/McGraw-Hill

THE SURPRISE FAMILY

everywhere   drink   afternoon   swim   farther   nest

Choose a word from the box to finish each sentence. Write the answers in the puzzle.

Across

2. The baby naps in the ___.

5. Ducks like to ___.

6. Trees can be found almost ___.

Down

1. I need a ___ of water.

3. Go a little ___ and you will find the pond.

4. How many eggs are in the ___?

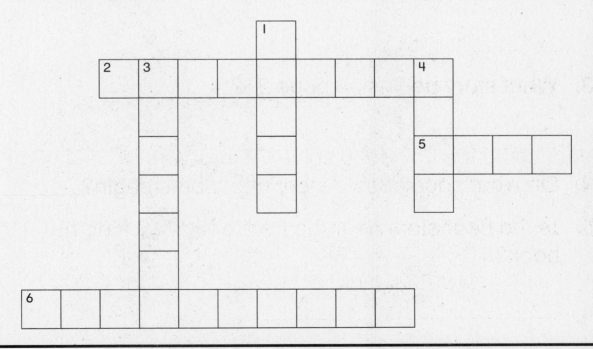

6

Level 4/Unit 2
Selection Vocabulary

Extension: Invite children to make a word search puzzle using the six words in the box.

231

SOLVE THE PROBLEM

Look at each picture. It shows a problem. Write two ways that the problem could be solved.

What could the girl do to solve the problem?

1. _____

_____

2. _____

_____

What could the boy do to solve the problem?

3. _____

_____

4. _____

Extension: Challenge children to draw a picture of a problem and to write two possible ways to solve it.

Level 4/Unit 2
ORGANIZE INFORMATION:
Problem and Solution

4

Macmillan/McGraw-Hill

WIDE WORDS

Read each sentence. Write the word that solves each riddle.

1. This is something you can do.   _____

       side   hide   wide

2. A street can be like this.   _____

       tide   ride   wide

3. You might see this in the park.   _____

       slide   tide   side

4. You can do this in a car.   _____

       wide   tide   ride

5. An ocean can have this.   _____

       slide   wide   tide

5   Level 4/Unit 2
Long Vowels and Phonograms /ī/ -ide

Extension: Invite children to choose two of the words and to write their own riddles for them. Classmates can write the missing word.

233

FAT CAT WORDS

Look at each picture. Write the two words that tell about the picture.

1. A _____ is sleeping on a _____.

   fat   cat   bat   mat

2. The _____ is hanging on a _____.

   hat   pat   cat   bat

3. That _____ is very _____.

   cat   rat   sat   fat

4. My sister _____ likes to _____.

   sat   Pat   chat   that

234   **Extension:** Challenge children to write two-word phrases using **-at** words. For example, *fat cat* or *Pat sat.*

Level 4/Unit 2
Short Vowels and Phonograms /a/ -at

4

Macmillan/McGraw-Hill

MAKE A STORY

Make up your own story. Choose one set of words
from each list. First, write how your story will end.
Then write your story. Write at least three sentences.

Where	**Who**	**Problem**
in the city	a boy and girl	a baby is missing
at a pond	a king and queen	someone has made a mess
in a castle	a hen and chicks	a new house is needed
in a house	a duck and a mouse	someone is sad

How will the problem be solved?

_____

_____

Now write your story.

_____

_____

_____

_____

_____

Level 4/Unit 2
4 **ANALYZE STORY ELEMENTS: Character,** **Extension:** Invite children to illustrate their stories and read them to
Plot, Setting classmates.

235

SWINGING WORDS

Say the name of each picture. Circle the word that begins with the same sound.

1. 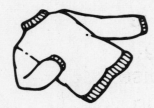   street   sweet   seven

2.    strange   song   swat

3.    swan   stop   space

4.    school   swamp   smile

5.    ship   sun   swallow

Extension: Direct children to write a story about one of the pictures. Invite them to read their story to a classmate.

Level 4/Unit 2
Consonant Blends /sw/ *sw*   5

Macmillan/McGraw-Hill

KEEP IT SHORT

Read each story. Then write one sentence that tells what the story is about.

1. A frog lived in the pond. He did not like it when the ducklings went swimming. They would splash him and make noise. He would croak at them. One duckling told him to hop on her back. The duckling gave the frog a ride. The frog had fun. After that, he played with the ducklings when they came to the pond.

_____

_____

2. All of Fuzzy Duckling's brothers and sisters could quack. Fuzzy Duckling could not. She tried and tried. One day her brother said, "Boo!" Fuzzy Duckling jumped and said, "Quack." Then everyone laughed. Fuzzy Duckling was happy.

_____

Extension: Invite children to give summaries of their favorite stories. Classmates can figure out the story that is being summarized.

ALIKE AND DIFFERENT

Name: _____ Date: _____

Show how a chick and a duckling are alike and how they are different. Read the words. Put an **X** under the name of the animal that each word or set of words tells about.

	Chick	Duckling
wings	_____	_____
pointed beak	_____	_____
feathers	_____	_____
webbed feet	_____	_____
two eyes	_____	_____
can swim	_____	_____
flat beak	_____	_____

Macmillan/McGraw-Hill

238

Extension: Invite children to write two sentences that tell how chicks and ducklings are alike and two that tell how they are different.

Level 4/Unit 2

ORGANIZE INFORMATION: Comparison and Contrast

10

REMEMBERING THE STORY

Underline the words that finish the sentence.

1. The boy showed the chick ____.
   how to find water and food
   how to fly and scratch

2. The boy gave the little hen ____.
   a soft nest
   a clutch of eggs

3. The boy and the little hen took
   the babies for a walk ____.
   in the yard
   around the garden

4. When the babies jumped into
   the water, the little hen ____.
   jumped into the water, too
   cried her danger cry

5. When the babies came back from
   their swim, the little hen ____.
   looked at them carefully
   danced her danger dance

Macmillan/McGraw-Hill

5   Level 4/Unit 2
Story Comprehension

Extension: Challenge children to write other sentences about the story
and to leave blanks for classmates to fill in.

239

PLAY DAY WORDS

Look at each picture. Write the letter or letters from the box that complete the name of each picture.

| d | cl | h | b | p | tr | pl | spr |

1.

_____ay

2.

_____ay

3.

_____ay

4.

_____ay

5.

_____ay

6.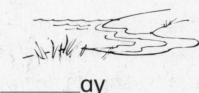

_____ay

7.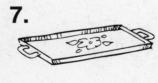

_____ay

8.

_____ay

Extension: Invite children to write sentences for five of the words. Classmates can underline the words that end in **ay**.

Level 4/Unit 2
Long Vowels and Phonograms /ā/ -ay

8

Macmillan/McGraw-Hill

SQUEAKY WORDS

Look at each picture. Write two words from the box to complete each sentence.

| square | squeeze | squirrel | squash |

1. Please do not _____ the _____.

2. The _____ is in the _____.

4

Level 4/Unit 2
Consonant Blends /skw/ *squ*

Extension: Challenge pairs of children to write other sentences in which they use two words that begin with the same sound as **squeak**.

241

READ AND DO

Look at the picture. Then read and follow the directions.

1. Color the third duckling yellow.

2. Write the word CROAK above the frog.

3. Put a square around the hen.

4. Draw leaves on the tree.

5. Number the ducklings 1, 2, 3, 4.

242   **Extension:** Challenge children to write one more direction that could be used with the picture on the page.

Level 4/Unit 2
Study Skills: Follow Directions
5

Macmillan/McGraw-Hill

Name: _____ Date: _____

UNIT VOCABULARY REVIEW

Look at the words in the box. Underline the word your teacher says.

1. pond pants pair	**2.** silly swim return	**3.** prince brother farther
4. queen turn king	**5.** great drink gave	**6.** nice nose knight
7. afternoon agree animals	**8.** cook clothes count	**9.** head whole woods
10. strange socks sister	**11.** everywhere elephant ears	**12.** visit nest legs
13. along beautiful afternoon	**14.** swim strange silly	**15.** fallen sister farther

Macmillan/McGraw-Hill

IN THE ATTIC

empty quiet toys share attic climbed

Circle the word that completes each sentence.
Then write the word.

1. Mother keeps old pictures in the _____ .
   share   attic

2. Be very _____! The baby is sleeping.
   quiet   climb

3. The cat _____ the tree.
   empty   climbed

4. She likes to play with her _____.
   toys   share

5. The _____ box is a good hiding place.
   empty   climb

6. Friends _____ their things.
   quiet   share

244 **Extension:** Have children choose a sentence and illustrate it.

Level 5/Unit 1
Selection Vocabulary
6

Macmillan/McGraw-Hill

PLEASING WORDS

Say the name of each picture. Then circle the picture in each row whose name begins with **pl**.

1.

2.

3.

4.

5.

Level 5/Unit 1
Consonant Blends /pl/ *pl*   **Extension:** Have children write sentences using the **pl** words.   **245**

5

THE MESSY ROOM

Read the story. Then fill in the circles in front of the correct answer.

    It was Saturday. It was time for Jack to clean his room. But Jack kept putting it off. Then, Joe came over to play. They went to the park. They played ball all day. When Jack came home, he ate a big dinner. Then he went to bed early.

I. Jack did not clean his room because he ____.
○ went to the park
○ read a book
○ walked his dog

2. When Jack came home from the park, he was ____.
○ excited   ○ sad   ○ hungry

3. Jack went to bed early because he was ____.
○ happy   ○ tired   ○ hungry

4. Did Jack like to clean his room?
○ yes   ○ no

246 **Extension:** Have students predict what Jack will do about his messy room.

Level 5/Unit 1
Make Inferences
4

Macmillan/McGraw-Hill

RHYMING -OLD WORDS

Read each sentence. Underline the **old** words.
Then choose one sentence and draw a picture to
go with it.

1. Fold the old blanket.

2. I told the man about the gold.

3. It is a cold day.

4. Father will scold the dog.

5. Max can hold the book.

SH-SH-SH

Choose the word from the box that completes each sentence. Write the word on the line.

shell	shoe	shed	ship	shelf

1. The _____ floats in the river.

2. He put his _____ on his foot.

3. The teacher put the books on the _____.

4. Chris found a _____ on the beach.

5. We put our bikes in the _____.

Extension: Have children choose one sentence and draw a picture to go with it.

Macmillan/McGraw-Hill

REAL OR MAKE-BELIEVE

Look at the picture and read the sentence. Circle each sentence that tells about something that really could happen.

1. Karen sits on a cloud and reads her book.

2. The mail carrier gives him a letter.

3. The camel drives the bus.

4. The duck washes the dishes.

5. Uncle Terry paints the fence.

6. We go for a walk in the park.

6
Level 5/Unit 1
Fantasy and Reality

Extension: Have children change the fantasy sentences into reality sentences and draw a picture to go with their new sentences.

249

Macmillan/McGraw-Hill

RITA AND RAMONA

Read each story. Then underline the sentence that makes sense with each story.

1. Rita lives in a red house.

She drives a red car.

She likes to eat apples and cherries.

Rita has red hair.

She grows red roses.

Red is Rita's favorite color.

Rita lives in the city.

2. Ramona has a dog.

She has two cats.

She has a bird and some goldfish.

Ramona works at the zoo.

Ramona likes to read.

Ramona likes animals.

Extension: Have children add more details to each story that would support each conclusion.

Level 5/Unit 1
Draw Conclusions

2

Macmillan/McGraw-Hill

IN THE ATTIC

Write the word that answers each question.

1. Did the boy go **up** or **down** to get to the attic?

_____

2. Did the boy find a family of **mice** or **cats** in the attic?

_____

3. Did the spider and the boy make a **cake** or a **web**?

_____

4. Did the boy find an old flying **machine** or a **car**?

_____

5. Was the boy's friend a **tiger** or a **kangaroo**?

_____

5

Level 5/Unit 1
Story Comprehension

Extension: Have children draw a picture of something they might see on a make-believe trip to an attic.

251

What Is It?

Look at the picture. Read the question. Write the answer.

I. Is this a **race** or a **face**? _____

2. Is this **lace** or a **place**? _____

3. Is this a **face** or a **space**? _____

4. Is this a **race** or a **brace**? _____

5. Is this a **face** or a **place**? _____

Extension: Have children follow the pattern presented on this page and create their own pictures and questions, using two **-ace** words. Have children exchange their work and answer each other's questions.

Level 5/Unit 1
Long Vowels and Phonograms /ā/ -ace

5

SAM THE SPIDER

spoon	spends	spot	spider	spins

Use the words in the box to tell a story about Sam.
Write the words on the lines.

1. Sam is a _____.

2. He _____ silk.

3. He makes his web in a special _____.

4. He _____ a lot of time making his web.
He also eats flies.

5. He never uses a _____.

5

Level 5/Unit 1
Consonant Blends /sp/ *sp*

Extension: Have children look in magazines for pictures of objects or
actions that begin with **sp**.

253

WHAT'S FOR DINNER?

Look at the pictures. Then follow the directions.

1. Underline the food you eat with a spoon.

2. Circle the foods that are not cooked.

3. Put an X on the foods you can eat
   with your fingers.

4 Write the letter **R** next to the food
   a rabbit likes to eat too.

5. Color the food you like the best.

254 **Extension:** Have children list foods they might eat for breakfast or lunch.

Level 5/Unit 1
Study Skills: Follow Directions

5

Macmillan/McGraw-Hill

Name: _____   Date: _____

JULIETA AND HER PAINTBOX

| color | storm | paint | remember | before | donkey |

Read each sentence. Underline the word in the sentence that is in the box. Then write the word on the line.

1. Wash your hands before lunch. _____

2. I remember where my shoe is. _____

3. The paint spilled on the floor. _____

4. Danita fed a carrot to the donkey. _____

5. What color is the car? _____

6. The storm caused a flood. _____

6

Level 5/Unit 1
Selection Vocabulary

Extension: Invite children to write a sentence using one of the words from the box and draw a picture to go with it.

255

FRED FOX

Read the story. Then answer the questions.

Fred Fox lives in the city.

He has a shiny red car.

He likes to drive his car.

He drives too fast.

Police Officer Ann gives him a ticket.

Now Fred Fox drives slowly.

1. Where does Fred Fox live? _____

2. Who drives too fast? _____

3. Who gives Fred Fox a ticket? _____

4. What does Fred do after he gets a ticket?

_____

256 Extension: Have children write words to describe Fred Fox.

Level 5/Unit 1
ANALYZE STORY ELEMENTS:
Character, Plot, Setting

4

SQUARE WORDS

Circle the pictures whose names begin with the same sound as **squint**. Write **squ** on the lines.

1. _____

2. _____

3. _____

4. _____

5. _____

6. _____

7. _____

8. _____

8 Level 5/Unit 1
Consonant Blends /skw/ *squ*

Extension: Have children write sentences about the pictures they circled.

257

IS THIS REAL?

Write **yes** or **no** to answer each question.

1. Can a  write a letter?   _____

2. Can a lay an egg?   _____

3. Can a  fly?   _____

4. Can you bake a cake in the  ?   _____

5. Can a  carry a baby in her pocket?

_____

6. Can a  jump?   _____

Extension: Divide children into two groups. Have one group tell about something real and the other group tell about something that is make-believe.

Level 5/Unit 1
Fantasy and Reality   6

Macmillan/McGraw-Hill

RHYME TIME

Look at each picture. Write the letters to complete
each word.

1. l _____

2. t _____

3. ch _____

4. d _____

5. gr _____

Macmillan/McGraw-Hill

5

Level 5/Unit 1
Long Vowels and Phonograms /ī/ -ime   **Extension:** Ask children to write or tell a story using **-ime** words.

259

JOAN'S SURPRISE

Read the story. Then use the picture to answer the questions.

Joan came home from school.
Dad said, "Go find Lucy."
Joan looked and looked.
She found Lucy.
She found a surprise, too.

1. Where does Joan live?

_____

2. Who tells Joan to look for Lucy?

_____

3. What kind of animal is Lucy?

_____

4. Where does Joan find Lucy?

_____

5. What is the surprise?

_____

Extension: Have children draw pictures showing what Joan did after
she found Lucy.

Macmillan/McGraw-Hill

WHO CAN HELP?

Read each sentence. Draw a line to the person who can help.

1. I want something to eat.

2. I have a toothache.

3. I want to cross the street.

4. I broke my leg.

5. The phone is not working.

5

Level 5/Unit 1
Make Inferences

Extension: Have children look through magazines to find pictures of other people who are helpers.

261

Macmillan/McGraw-Hill

DOES IT BELONG?

Choose a word from the word box that belongs with each group. Write the word on the line.

tree	six	dime	blue	dog	moon

1. red, green, _____

2. stars, sun, _____

3. two, four, _____

4. penny, nickel, _____

5. cat, bird, _____

6. flower, grass, _____

Macmillan/McGraw-Hill

JULIETA AND HER PAINTBOX

Underline the sentence that tells about the story.
Then draw a line to the picture.

1. Julieta had a paintbox.

Julieta had a box of crayons.

2. The city was big.

The city looked
like a checkerboard.

3. Julieta painted snowflakes.

Julieta painted clouds
and raindrops.

4. Julieta painted a red tiger.

Julieta painted a green donkey.

5. Julieta painted her house.

Julieta painted what she saw
in her dream.

-USE WORDS

| fuse | amuse | use | excuse |

Look at each picture. Choose a word from the box to complete the sentence. Write the word on the line.

1. You can _____ my pen.

2. Please _____ me.

3. Here is the _____ box.

4. Can the boy _____ the baby?

Macmillan/McGraw-Hill

Extension: Have students make up their own sentences using the words from the box.

Level 5/Unit 1
Long Vowels and Phonograms /ū/ -use
4

Name: _____ Date: _____

STRONG WORDS

Look at the picture. Say the name of the picture.
Write the missing letters on the line.

1. Mother took the baby for a walk
in the _____ oller.

2. He drinks milk through a _____ aw.

3. The cat plays with the _____ ing.

4. Look both ways before crossing
the _____ eet.

5. The girl wades in the _____ eam.

Macmillan/McGraw-Hill

Extension: Have children think of other words that begin with the same
sound as **strong**. Then have them draw a picture for one of the words.

STEP BY STEP

Read the directions. Do what each sentence tells you to do.

1. Draw a line from the sun to the moon.

2. Put an X on the drum.

3. Circle the turtle.

4. Draw a box around the clown.

5. Draw two lines from the bee to its house.

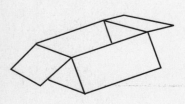

6. Draw something you can put in the empty box.

266 **Extension:** Have children give oral directions for a simple task.

Level 5/Unit 1
Study Skills: Follow Directions
6

Macmillan/McGraw-Hill

JIMMY LEE DID IT

| mystery finally capture pictures guess crayons |

Write the word from the box that matches the clue.

1. to trap something _____

2. something you can draw _____

3. to not know for sure _____

4. things used for coloring _____

5. at the end _____

6. something unknown _____

6 Level 5/Unit 1
Selection Vocabulary

Extension: Have children use selection vocabulary words in their own sentences.

267

NAME THAT PICTURE

Say the name of the picture. Then write a word
from the box that tells about the picture.

name	game	tame	frame	same

1.

a picture in a _____

2.

a _____ of checkers

3.

two of the _____ bears

4.

the boy's _____

5.

a _____ animal

268   **Extension:** Have children write a poem using **-ame** words.

Level 5/Unit 1

Long Vowels and Phonograms /ā/ -ame

5

Macmillan/McGraw-Hill

FUNNY MONDAY

Read the story. Then write an X next to the sentences that tell about make-believe things.

1. _____ I went to school on Monday.

2. _____ I met a space girl.

3. _____ I read a good book at school.

4. _____ I took a test.

5. _____ A tiger gave the test.

6. _____ I went home on a spaceship.

Manuel's Birthday

Read the story. Think about which sentences tell
something important about the story. Underline
those sentences.

Today is Manuel's birthday.

He is seven years old.

He is very tall.

Mother has baked him a cake.

She puts it on a round plate.

Father has put up a piñata.

The piñata has a flower on its side.

At Manuel's party, friends hit the piñata.

The piñata is blue.

The piñata breaks and everyone grabs the prizes.

Extension: Have children write sentences that add important
information to the story.

Level 5/Unit 1
Important and Unimportant Information
6

Macmillan/McGraw-Hill

WHAT DO YOU THINK?

Read the sentences. Think about how the person feels. Circle the word that tells how the person might feel.

1. Pelamo wants a new toy.
   His mom says no.
   Pelamo is _____.
   sad   happy   excited

2. Anna loves animals.
   Dad brings her a hamster.
   Anna is _____.
   sad   mad   happy

3. Pedro wants a snack.
   He asks for an apple.
   Pedro is _____.
   silly   hungry   happy

4. Dad looks at the clock.
   He yawns.
   Dad is _____.
   sad   happy   sleepy

Macmillan/McGraw-Hill

CLIMB THE STEPS

Circle the picture that names a word that begins
with the same sound as **steps.** Then write the word
on the line.

stem	sting	stone	stick	stack

1. _____

2. _____

3. _____

4. _____

5. _____

272 **Extension:** Have children write sentences using the **st** words.

Level 5/Unit 1
Consonant Blends /st/ *st*   5

Name: _____   Date: _____

CAN YOU TELL WHY?

The picture shows what happened. If the sentence
tells why it happened, write **yes**.

1. It is snowing.   _____

2. The car has a flat tire.   _____

3. It is a hot day.   _____

4. The runner wins the race.   _____

5. It is Aunt Lucia's birthday.   _____

6. The ball is in the bushes.   _____

TIC-TAC-TOE

Put an X through words that do not rhyme with
made. Write the words that are left on the lines.

frame	fade	care
ship	shade	cape
smash	face	grade

1. _____

2. _____

3. _____

trade	train	time
cake	blade	map
same	some	wade

4. _____

5. _____

6. _____

Macmillan/McGraw-Hill

BE A WORD DETECTIVE!

Read each story. Look at the underlined word.
Then write the word in the story that helps you
know the meaning of the underlined word.

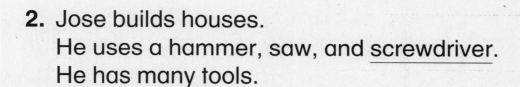

1. Jay goes to the store.
   He likes fruit.
   He buys apples, bananas, and <u>grapes</u>.

   _____

2. Jose builds houses.
   He uses a hammer, saw, and <u>screwdriver</u>.
   He has many tools.

   _____

3. Grandpa has a big garden.
   He grows many kinds of flowers.
   He grows roses, lilies, and <u>tulips</u>.

   _____

4. Marie paints pictures.
   She uses special paint.
   She paints with <u>watercolors</u>.

   _____

Macmillan/McGraw-Hill

Extension: Have children look through their books to find an unfamiliar word. Help them use the context of the sentence to figure out the meaning of the word.

JIMMY LEE DID IT

Color the pictures that show what Jimmy Lee did.

1.

2.

3.

4.

5.

6.

276 **Extension:** Help children think of other ways to tell about Jimmy Lee.

Level 5/Unit 1
Story Comprehension   6

Macmillan/McGraw-Hill

A LINE OF -INE WORDS

Look at each picture. Draw a line to the sentence
that tells about the picture. Underline the **ine** word
in each sentence.

I.    These shoes are not mine.

2.    On warm days we dine outside.

3.    The nest is in the pine tree.

4.    The children stand in line.

5.    Today I am nine.

Macmillan/McGraw-Hill

5

Level 5/Unit 1
Long Vowels and Phonograms: /ī/ -ine

Extension: Have children write and illustrate sentences with **-ine** words in them.

277

Name: _____   Date: _____

Sprinkler Words

Circle the pictures that have the same beginning sound as **spruce**. Then write a word from the box under each **spr** picture.

| spread | sprout | spray | spring | sprinkler |

1.

_____

2.

_____

3.

_____

4

_____

5.

_____

6.

_____

7.

_____

8.

_____

Extension: Have children write sentences using some of the **spr** words.

Level 5/Unit 1

Consonant Blends /spr/ *spr*

8

Macmillan/McGraw-Hill

Name: Date:

NEW SHOES FOR SILVIA

Circle a word to complete each sentence.

1.

The teacher gave ＿＿ a pencil.
present   everyone

2.

The yo-yo has a long ＿＿.
letter   string

3.

We ＿＿ stickers.
collected   shoes

4.

Please mail this ＿＿.
letter   string

5.

Raul can tie his own ＿＿.
shoes   present

6.

Mai opened the ＿＿.
letter   present

Macmillan/McGraw-Hill

6   Level 5/Unit 1
Selection Vocabulary

Extension: Have children write their own sentences using selection vocabulary words.

279

RECESS TIME

Read the story. Then put the pictures in the correct order by numbering the boxes.

Mr. Lopez's class goes out for recess.
First, the children jump rope.
Next, they play ball.
Then, they go on the swings.
Finally, Mr. Lopez says, "It's time to go in."

Extension: Have children draw pictures to show the order of events in their school day.

ORGANIZE INFORMATION: Sequence of Events

Level 5/Unit 1

4

Macmillan/McGraw-Hill

WHAT IS IT?

Look at the picture. Read the question. Write the answer.

1. Does the baby **weep** or **creep?** _____

2. Does the girl **sleep** or **sweep?** _____

3. Is the hill **steep** or **beep**? _____

4. Is this a **jeep** or a **sheep**? _____

5. Is the hole **peep** or **deep**? _____

Macmillan/McGraw-Hill

5

Level 5/Unit 1
Long Vowels and Phonograms /ē/ -eep

Extension: Have children write sentences using some of the **eep** words.

281

TROLL TIME

Unscramble the mixed up letters to make a word that ends in **ine**.

dine	pine	nine	mine	line

1.  The troll says, "This forest is **inem**."

_____

2.  I have many **inep** trees.

_____

3.  They grow in a straight **niel**.

_____

4.  I have **inne** books.

_____

5.  We always **ined** together.

_____

282 **Extension:** Have children write sentences using the **ine** words.

Level 5/Unit 1
Long Vowels and Phonograms /ī/ -ine

5

Macmillan/McGraw-Hill

Riddle Time

Read the clues. Write a word from the box to solve the riddle.

stroller	string	stripe	street	straw

1. I am part of a city.
Cars go on me.

I am a _____.

2. I am thin and strong.
I am tied to a kite.

I am a _____.

3. I can be thick or thin.
You can see me on a zebra.

I am a _____.

4. I am made of paper or plastic.
You use me to drink milk.

I am a _____.

5. I have wheels.
A baby sits in me.

I am a _____.

5

Level 5/Unit 1
Consonant Blends /str/ *str*

Extension: Have children look through magazines to find pictures of things whose names begin with **str**.

283

ADDING -ING

Read each sentence. Write the word that completes the sentence.

jump   jumping

1. The girl is _____ over the stream.

2. The girl will _____ over the stream.

cook   cooking

3. Father will _____ the chicken.

4. Father is _____ the chicken.

wash   washing

5. Don will _____ the car.

6. Don is _____ the car.

Extension: Have children list action words, add **ing** to each word, and then use the **-ing** word in a sentence.

Level 5/Unit 1
Inflectional Endings *-ing*   6

Macmillan/McGraw-Hill

A DAY WITH KAY

Read the story. Then, read the questions and circle the picture that tells about Kay.

It is a sunny summer day.
Kay is having fun with her friends.
Dad calls Kay home for lunch.
Kay does not want to go home.
Dad tells Kay to put the plates on the table.
Kay drops a plate.
Kay is upset.

1. How does Kay feel when she plays with her friends?

2. How does Kay feel when Dad calls her home for lunch?

3. How does Kay feel when she drops the plate?

4. Where does Kay drop the plate?

A BIRTHDAY SURPRISE

Read the story. Underline the answer to the question.

Today is Mother's birthday.
Will and Jill have a surprise for Mother.
Will picks flowers.
Jill makes toast.
Jill pours the juice.
Will carries the tray to Mother's bed.
Will and Jill say, "Happy Birthday, Mother."

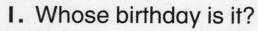

1. Whose birthday is it?

Bill's   Jill's   Mother's

2. Who picks the flowers?

Mother   Will   Bill

3. What does Jill make?

toast   eggs   tea

4. Where is Mother?

outside   in the kitchen   in bed

5. How does Mother feel?

sad   happy   sick

Extension: Have children tell a story about a birthday surprise for a family member.

Level 5/Unit 1
Summarize

5

Macmillan/McGraw-Hill

NEW SHOES FOR SILVIA

Read the sentences. Underline the answers that tell about the story.

1. What does Tía Rosita send Silvia?

   a book   new shoes   a doll

2. What color are the new shoes?

   blue   black   red

3. The shoes are not right for Silvia. They are _____.

   too big   too small

4. Silvia uses the shoes to _____.

   make doll beds   hold candy   carry crayons

5. Silvia uses the shoes to make a _____.

   basket   two-car train   umbrella

6. Where does Silvia wear her new shoes?

   the post office   the school   the store

 6   Level 5/Unit 1
Story Comprehension

Extension: Have children draw pictures to show what happened in the story.

287

Macmillan/McGraw-Hill

FIND THE RIGHT WORD

Circle the word that completes each sentence.

1. These shoes are too ____.

tight   sight

2. I see the moon at ____.

night   light

3. He holds the pencil in his ____ hand.

sight   right

4. The candle had a ____ flame.

might   bright

5. He turned on the bedroom ____.

sight   light

288   **Extension:** Have children write words and draw pictures that tell about the **night**.

Level 5/Unit 1
Long Vowels and Phonograms /ī/ -*ight* 5

PATRICK THE PIG

Look at the picture. Underline the word that completes the sentence. Write the word.

1. Patrick is a _____ pig.

smash   smart

2. He can _____ acorns
miles way.

smooth   smell

3. Patrick will _____
the acorns.

smash   smart

4. Then he eats the _____
acorns.

smoke   small

5. Tasty acorns make Patrick

_____.

smile   smoke

UNIT VOCABULARY REVIEW

Look at the words in the box. Underline the word your teacher says.

1. queen quiet crayons	**2.** shoes pair share	**3.** everywhere empty elephant
4. color collect cook	**5.** strange string swim	**6.** before return remember
7. clothes capture climbed	**8.** finally farther elephant	**9.** guess nest great
10. visit present pants	**11.** mother mystery sister	**12.** attic afternoon agree
13. before brother storm	**14.** pants paint picture	**15.** storm strange turn

JUST A LITTLE BIT

| against | board | crowd | someone | watch | hard |

Follow the directions.

1. Draw a picture of someone who wears a uniform.

2. Draw a picture of something you watch.

3. Draw a picture of something made from a board.

4. Draw a picture of a crowd.

5. Draw a picture of something hard.

6. Draw a picture of something leaning against something else.

6

Level 5
Selection Vocabulary

Extension: Have children write sentences about two of the pictures they drew.

291

FLY, SPY, OR CRY?

Look at the picture. Read the question. Write the answer.

1. Is this a **fly** or a **spy**? _____

2. Is this the **sky** or a **spy**? _____

3. Does the cook **dry** or **fry** the chicken? _____

4. Does the baby **pry** or **cry**? _____

5. Will the clothes **fry** or **dry**? _____

292 **Extension:** Have children write sentences for the words they didn't write.

Level 5/Unit 2
Long Vowels and Phonograms /ī/ y   5

Macmillan/McGraw-Hill

IS IT YOURS?

Look at the pictures. Write the name of the person and **'s** to show who the thing belongs to.

 TOM

 JUAN

1. _____ hat

2. _____ dog

 MOM

 MS. CLARK

3. _____ cat

4. _____ book

 PATTY

 BRAD

5. _____ bike

6. _____ umbrella

6
Level 5/Unit 2
STRUCTURAL CLUES: Possessives

Extension: Have children write other possessive phrases using names of family members.

293

Macmillan/McGraw-Hill

WHAT COMES FIRST?

Number the pictures 1, 2, and 3 to show what happened first, next, and last.

1.

   _____ _____ _____

2.

   _____ _____ _____

3.

   _____ _____ _____

4.

   _____ _____ _____

Extension: Have children draw a picture of something that could happen next in each situation.

Level 5/Unit 2
ORGANIZE INFORMATION: Sequence of Events

4

Name: _____ Date: _____

SUSIE'S HOUSE

Use the pictures and sentences to help you figure out what the underlined word means. Circle the answer.

1. Susie's mother has beautiful dishes she keeps in a <u>cabinet</u> in the dining room. A cabinet is ___

a piece of furniture.   a place to sleep.

2. Susie's grandmother made a <u>quilt</u> for Susie's bed. A quilt is ___

a fruit.   a blanket.

3. Susie and her dad make bread and <u>biscuits</u>. A biscuit is ___

something you bake.   something you sit on.

4. Susie's mother uses a hose, rake, and <u>trowel</u> in her garden. A trowel is ___

a thing to wear.   a garden tool.

Macmillan/McGraw-Hill

4 Level 5
Unfamiliar Words

Extension: Have children write their own sentences using the unfamiliar words.

295

Name: _____ Date: _____

WHERE IS IT?

Look at the picture. Then circle the answer to each question.

1. Where is the  ?

on the shelf   under the table   on top of the box

2. What is on the shelf?

3. What is next to the glass?

4. Where is the ?

on top of the chest   on the shelf   on the floor

Extension: Have children write about where things are in a room at home.

Level 5
Spatial Relationships

4

Macmillan/McGraw-Hill

SUM IT UP

Read each story. Write one sentence that tells what the story is about.

Gus had a dog named Jake. Gus taught Jake to do many tricks. A man came to see Jake do his tricks. He took Jake to the city. You can see Jake do tricks on his television show.

_____

_____

Jordan sent letters to every boy and girl in the class. He brought balloons to school. Anna's mother baked a cake. When the teacher came into the room, everyone said, "Surprise!"

_____

_____

2 Level 5/Unit 2
Summarize

Extension: Have children work in pairs to write a one-sentence summary for a story they know.

297

Macmillan/McGraw-Hill

Name: _____   Date: _____

USE YOUR SKULL!

Look at the picture. Then draw a line to the sentence
that tells about the picture.

1.   Jim's skate has a missing wheel.

2.    The skunk surprised the bear.

3.    Sadie likes to skip during recess.

4.    Your skull protects your brain.

5.    There is a rainbow in the sky.

298   **Extension:** Have children circle all the words that begin with the same
sound as **skill**.

FIND THE SOLUTION

Read the sentences that tell the problem. Then write a sentence that tells a solution.

1. Problem: Michelle has to walk her dog before school. Often, she misses the bus.

Solution: _____

_____

2. Problem: Ben plays baseball. He falls and tears his shirt. He needs his shirt for the game on Friday.

Solution: _____

_____

3. Problem: Betty forgets her spelling book. She has spelling homework.

Solution: _____

_____

4. Problem: Keith can't find his watch. He knows it is in his bedroom. His bedroom is messy.

Solution: _____

_____

4 | Level 5
Problem and Solution

Extension: Divide children into two groups. Have one group write problems; the other group can write solutions.

Name: _____   Date: _____

JUST A LITTLE BIT

Underline the sentence that tells about the story.
Then draw a line to the picture.

1. Elephant and Mouse
were at the park.
Elephant and Mouse
were at the store.

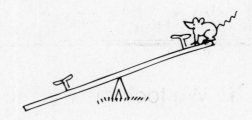

2. Elephant and Mouse
sat on the slide.
Elephant and Mouse
sat on the seesaw.

3. Mouse made the seesaw
go up and down.
Mouse could not make
the seesaw go up and down.

4. Giraffe, Zebra, and Lion
sat with Elephant.
Giraffe, Zebra, and Lion
sat with Mouse.

Extension: Have children discuss other situations where "every little
bit helps."

Level 5
Story Comprehension

8

Macmillan/McGraw-Hill

A TRIP TO TOWN

Write a word from the box to complete each sentence.

clown	crown	frown	town	gown

1. We took the train to _____.

2. My sister bought a new _____.

3. Mom would not buy her a gold _____.

4. My sister began to _____.

5. Mom bought me a funny _____.

Macmillan/McGraw-Hill

USE YOUR EARS!

Name: Date:

Say the name of the picture. Circle the letters that stand for the beginning sound of the picture name.

1.

  cr   fr

2.

  cr   fr

3.

  cr   fr

4.

  cr   fr

5.

  cr   fr

6.

  cr   fr

7.

  cr   fr

8.

  cr   fr

Extension: Have children look in magazines for pictures whose names begin with **fr** and **cr**, and paste them on two separate posters labeled **fr** words and **cr** words.

Level 5
Consonant Blends /kr/ cr, /fr/ fr

8

A BIRTHDAY BASKET FOR TÍA

Read the clues. Then write a word from the box to complete the puzzle.

breakfast	party	fruit	secret	basket	birthday

Across
3. the day you were born
4. a woven container
6. something you don't tell

Down
1. a morning meal
2. a celebration
5. apples, oranges, bananas

Macmillan/McGraw-Hill

6

Level 5/Unit 2
Selection Vocabulary

Extension: Have children write a birthday story using the selection vocabulary words.

303

THE THIRTEEN THIMBLES

Read the story. Underline the words that begin with
th. Then write the words that match each picture.

Once, a thin girl named Thelma had thirteen

thimbles. Each day she put one on her thumb. A

thief took her thimbles. He ran into a thick

bush. He got a thorn in his thumb.

_____   _____

_____   _____

304   **Extension:** Have children write sentences for the pictured **th** words.

Level 5/Unit 2
Consonant Digraphs /th/ *th*   14

1–2–3 ORDER

Read the sentences. Write 1, 2, 3 to tell what happens first, next, and last.

1. ____ The bees were angry.

____ The bear climbed the tree.

____ The bear took the honey.

2. ____ The boy makes the kite.

____ The boy flies the kite.

____ The boy ties the string to the kite.

3. ____ Charlie mailed the letter.

____ Charlie wrote a letter to Grandpa.

____ Grandpa reads the letter.

4. ____ Mary ate breakfast.

____ Mary rode the bus to school.

____ Mary worked in the classroom.

4   Level 5
Sequence of Events

Extension: Have children rewrite sentences, using the words **first**, **next**, and **last**.

305

MAKE A WORD

Write **ace** to finish the word. Circle the picture the
word names.

1. f_____

2. l_____

3. r_____

 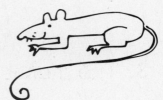

4. sp_____

5. br_____

Extension: Have children write sentences using three of the **-ace** words.

Macmillan/McGraw-Hill

OVER AND UNDER WORDS

Look at the picture. Write a word from the box to complete the sentence.

under	front	on	over	in	behind

1. The flag is in _____ of the school.

2. The ladybug is _____ the leaf.

3. The man is _____ the boys.

4. The bird is _____ the cage.

5. The slippers are _____ the bed.

6. The light is _____ the table.

Macmillan/McGraw-Hill

6 Level 5/Unit 2
ORGANIZE INFORMATION:
Spatial Relationships

Extension: Have children walk around the classroom and point out the location of different objects.

307

RAP RHYMES

Circle the pictures whose names rhyme with **rap**.
Then write the words.

wrap	lap	clap	cap	map	snap

1.  _____

2.  _____

3. _____

4. _____

5. _____

6.  _____

7.  _____

8. _____

308 **Extension:** How many other -**ap** words can children think of?

Level 5/Unit 2
Short Vowels and Phonograms /a/-*ap*

8

Macmillan/McGraw-Hill

DO YOU KNOW THE WORD?

Use the sentence to figure out the meaning of
the underlined word. Circle the correct meaning.
Then draw a picture of the word.

1. Shamir decorated the room for the
party. He hung up balloons, flowers,
and <u>streamers</u>.
long pieces of colored paper
pictures of animals
brightly colored candles

2. Aunt Vicki put a <u>platter</u> of chicken on
the table.
a pitcher
a large serving dish
a sharp knife

3. Hank picked a <u>bouquet</u> of roses.
yellow grass
newly planted seeds
a bunch of flowers

4. We waited for the train at the <u>station</u>.
a place where animals live
a place to buy clothes
a stopping place

Can You Guess What Happens?

Look at the pictures. Fill in the circle in front of the sentence that tells what will happen.

1.

○ The man will go on a trip.

○ There will be a party.

2.

○ The woman will put the plant on the table.

○ The woman will water the plant.

3.

○ Dad will take a nap.

○ Dad will get the ladder.

4.

○ She will go another way.

○ She will sit in the car.

Extension: Have children draw pictures of their predictions for one of the situations.

Level 5
Make, Confirm, or Revise Predictions

4

Macmillan/McGraw-Hill

A LOST PAL

Read the story. Then draw a line to finish each sentence.

Antonio went to visit Grandma and Grandpa. He flew on an airplane. Antonio took his special toy bear, Pete, to the airport.

Antonio does not know where Pete is. One day a box comes for Antonio. Antonio opens the box. Antonio is happy.

1. Antonio was excited   he sees Pete.

2. Pete is a   because he was going
                                          to visit his grandparents.

3. Antonio was worried   toy bear.

4. When Antonio   because Pete was
        opens the box   lost.

A Birthday Present for Tía

Read the sentence. Circle the word that completes the sentence.

1. It is _____ birthday.

Cecilia's   Chica's   Tía's

2. Tía is _____ years old.

ninety   nine   nineteen

3. Chica is a _____.

grandmother   girl   cat

4. Cecilia makes a birthday _____ for Tía.

hat   basket   necklace

5. Cecilia puts a _____ into the basket.

mixing bowl   book   crayon

6. Cecilia decorates Tía's basket with _____.

beads   ribbons   flowers

Extension: Have children list what they would put into a birthday basket for a special family member.

Macmillan/McGraw-Hill

THE TROUT SCOUT

Read the story. Then write a word from the box to complete each sentence.

pout	scout	out	trout

1. Tad is a _____.

2. Each morning, Tad takes

his boat _____.

3. He looks for _____.

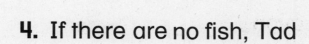

4. If there are no fish, Tad

will _____.

4   Level 5/Unit 2
Diphthongs and Phonograms /ou/ -out

Extension: Challenge children to write riddles using **-out** words and exchange them with classmates to solve.

313

Name: _____   Date: _____

Throw or Twist?

Say the name of the picture. Some pictures begin with the same sound as **throw**. Some pictures begin with the same sound as **twist**. Underline the letters that stand for the beginning sound of the name of the picture.

1. tw   thr

2. tw   thr

3. tw   thr

4. tw   thr

5. tw   thr

6. tw   thr

7. tw   thr

8. tw   thr

Extension: Have children write a sentence using one **thr** word and one **tw** word.

Level 5/Unit 2
Consonant Blends /tw/ *tw*, /thr/ *thr*   8

Macmillan/McGraw-Hill

WHAT DOES IT MEAN?

capture **Capture** means to catch and hold a person, animal, or thing.

chicken A **chicken** is a bird raised for food. A hen or a rooster is a **chicken**.

collect **Collect** means to bring together or gather together in a set. My brother likes to **collect** stamps.

cupboard A **cupboard** is a closet with shelves to store dishes or food.

Use the dictionary page above to answer the questions.

1. Can you capture a fly? _____

2. What can you eat? _____

3. Do you sleep in a cupboard? _____

4. Can you collect shells? _____

5. Is a hen a chicken? _____

5

Level 5/Unit 2
Reference Sources: Dictionary

Extension: Have children write sentences using each dictionary entry word.

315

GUINEA PIGS DON'T READ BOOKS

apples	fur	sniff	carrots	smell	chew

Read the question. Write *yes* or *no* to answer the question.

1. Does a rabbit eat carrots?   _____

2. Does a turtle have fur?   _____

3. Do apples grow on trees?   _____

4. Can you smell a rose?   _____

5. Do you chew milk?   _____

6. Do you sniff with your ears?   _____

316

Extension: Have children make up other questions about the selection vocabulary.

Level 5/Unit 2
Selection Vocabulary   6

Macmillan/McGraw-Hill

PICK OUT THE RIGHT WORD

Read each sentence. Write a word from the box to complete the sentence.

trout	shout	scout	out	pout

1. The man will _____ to his friends.

2. It is not good to _____.

3. The _____ swam in the river.

4. She took the papers _____ of her book bag.

5. The _____ put up the tent.

5

Level 5/Unit 2
Diphthongs and Phonograms /ou/ -out   Extension: Have children write a story using **-out** words.

317

SMILE WORDS

Read the definition. Write the **sm** word that goes with the definition. Then write a sentence for each word.

smash	small	smell	smile

1. little in size _____

_____

2. to break into pieces _____

_____

3. to sniff _____

_____

4. a happy look on the face _____

_____

318   **Extension:** Have children list other words that begin with **sm**.

Level 5/Unit 2
Consonant Blends /sm/ *sm*
8

Macmillan/McGraw-Hill

CITY LIVING

Read the story to find out how Sandy and Mandy
are alike and different.

Sandy and Mandy both live in the city. Sandy lives
in a tall apartment building with her mom and dad.
Mandy lives in a house with her mom and dad. Both
girls love flowers. Sandy grows flowers on her
balcony, but Mandy grows flowers in her yard.

Now read each sentence below. If it tells about
Sandy, write **Sandy** on the line. If it tells about
Mandy, write **Mandy**. If it tells about both girls,
write **both**.

1. She lives in the city. _____
2. She grows flowers. _____
3. She lives in an apartment building. _____
4. She has a yard. _____
5. She has a balcony. _____
6. She lives in a house. _____
7. She lives with her mom and dad. _____
8. She loves flowers. _____

8

Level 5/Unit 2
**ORGANIZE INFORMATION: Comparison
and Contrast**

Extension: Have children list other ways that Sandy and Mandy could
be alike and different.

319

Macmillan/McGraw-Hill

SUMMERTIME

Read the story.

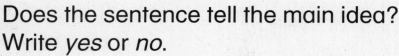

We go swimming at the beach.
We catch fireflies at night.
We eat watermelon.
We play games with our friends.
We have lots of fun each summer.

Does the sentence tell the main idea?
Write *yes* or *no*.

1. We eat watermelon. _____

2. We play games with our friends. _____

3. We have lots of fun each summer. _____

4. We go swimming at the beach. _____

5. We catch fireflies at night. _____

6. Write the sentence that tells the main idea.

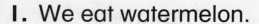

_____

Macmillan/McGraw-Hill

320 **Extension:** Have children write about things they do each summer.

Level 5/Unit 2
**ORGANIZE INFORMATION: Main Idea
and Supporting Details**

6

WHAT DO YOU THINK?

Read each story. Then underline the best conclusion.

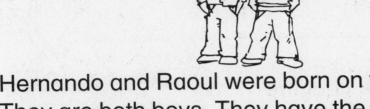

Hernando and Raoul were born on the same day. They are both boys. They have the same mother and father.

     Hernando and Raoul are twins.

     Hernando and Raoul are cousins.

Angelina's grandparents live far away. They live in Italy. Italy is across a big ocean. Angelina's grandparents are coming to visit.

     They will come in a car.

     They will come on an airplane.

Tom has a pet named Spot. Tom can hold Spot in his hand.

     Spot is a dog.

     Spot is a mouse.

Suzanne plays a musical instrument. It has strings.

     Suzanne plays the guitar.

     Suzanne plays the drum.

4 | Level 5/Unit 2
Draw Conclusions

Extension: Have children write stories and exchange with classmates to draw conclusions.

321

Name: _____   Date: _____

PLUG IN THE WORD

Read the clues. Then write a word from the box to complete each sentence.

rug	hug	bug	mug	plug

1. A puppy and a teddy bear are

   things you _____.

2. A chair and a couch are

   things on a _____.

3. A TV and a toaster are

   things with a _____.

4. Milk and apple juice are

   things in a _____.

5. A grasshopper is a

   kind of _____.

Macmillan/McGraw-Hill

GUINEA PIGS DON'T READ BOOKS

Read each sentence. Write **T** if the sentence is
true. Write **F** if the sentence is false.

1. _____ Guinea pigs can count.

2. _____ Guinea pigs eat apples and carrots.

3. _____ Guinea pigs will chew your toys.

4. _____ Guinea pigs do not see.

5. _____ Guinea pigs can sing.

6. _____ Guinea pigs can whistle.

7. _____ Guinea pigs have fur coats.

8. _____ All guinea pigs are brown.

9. _____ Guinea pigs are just like pigs that
live on a farm.

10. _____ A guinea pig is a good pet.

Macmillan/McGraw-Hill

10

Level 5/Unit 2
Story Comprehension

Extension: Have children list qualities that make a guinea pig a
good pet.

323

SOUND-ALIKE WORDS

Read the question. Write **ound** to complete the word. Circle the picture that answers the question.

1. What is r_____?

 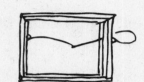 

2. What could be f_____ by a pirate?

3. What weighs a p_____?

4. What makes a s_____?

5. Which one is a h_____?

Extension: Have children suggest other answers for questions 1 and 4.

Diphthongs and Phonograms ou/ -ound

Level 5/Unit 2

5

Name: _____ Date: _____

SNEEZE WORDS

Look at the picture. Read the question. Write the answer.

I. Did the girl **sneeze** or **snoop**?

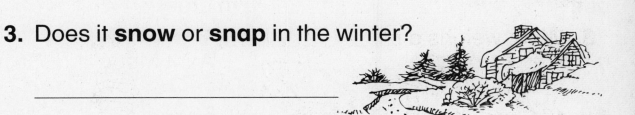

_____

2. Is this a **snake** or a **snail**?

_____

3. Does it **snow** or **snap** in the winter?

_____

4. Will she **snip** or **sneak** the paper?

_____

5. Is popcorn a tasty **snap** or **snack**?

_____

5

Level 5/Unit 2
Consonant Blends /sn/ *sn*

Extension: Have children look through their books for other words that begin with **sn** and make a list.

325

Macmillan/McGraw-Hill

A LETTER TO AMY

Write words from the box to finish the letter.

special	wish	envelope	stamp	store	inviting

Dear Jill,

Aunt Mary's birthday is next Sunday. I am

_____ the whole family. I want the

party to be very _____. I'm ordering

a big cake from the _____. Aunt Mary

loves to write letters. So the cake will have an

_____ with a _____ on it!

I hope you can come. I _____ I could

see you right now.

Love,

Bonnie

Extension: Have children write a letter to Bonnie from Jill accepting the invitation.

Level 5/Unit 2
Selection Vocabulary

6

Macmillan/McGraw-Hill

THINK AND DRAW

Write the word that completes each sentence. Then draw a picture of the word.

| spider | spoon | spade | spot | sponge |

1. Pedro ate his soup

with a _____.

2. The _____ made a

web in the corner.

3. She used a _____

to dig in the garden.

4. Maria had a _____

on her dress.

5. Andy used a _____

to wipe up the water.

5

Level 5/Unit 2
Consonant Blends /sp/ *sp*   Extension: Have children make up riddles for some of the **sp** words.   **327**

Macmillan/McGraw-Hill

A NEW HOUSE

Write a word from the box to complete the
sentence. Then read the story.

| down | crown | brown | town | frown |

A _____ horse and a duck lived in a barn.

A strong wind came.

It blew the barn _____ .

"What will we do?" said the duck.

"We will go to _____ ," said the horse.

The horse and the duck went to see the king.

The king had a gold _____ .

The king said, "Do not _____ . You
can live in my castle."

And they did.

328 **Extension:** Have children make up simple rhymes using -*own* words.

Level 5/Unit 2
Diphthongs and Phonograms /ou/ -*own*   5

Macmillan/McGraw-Hill

WHAT'S FOR DINNER?

Read the clues. Then draw a line to the correct picture.

1. I swim in the water.
You can cook me in a
pan or on a grill.

2. I am little and round.
I am a vegetable.
I am green.

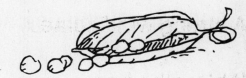

3. I am long and orange.
I grow under the ground.
You can eat me cooked or raw.

4. I am white and fluffy.
People all over the world eat me.

5. I can be made from different
kinds of greens.
I can have tomatoes and lettuce.

5   Level 5/Unit 2
Draw Conclusions

Extension: Have children write breakfast riddles to exchange with classmates.

329

Macmillan/McGraw-Hill

NEW IDEAS

Read each story and think about what will happen.
Then think about the new information and change
what you think will happen.

1. Lin wants to make a bed for her new puppy.
   What will she use?
   Lin will use a box.
   Lin cannot find a box.
   What will she use now?

_____

_____

2. It is Grandpa's birthday. What will Toby
   give him for a present?
   Toby will buy Grandpa a book.
   Toby cannot get to the store.
   What will Toby do now?

_____

_____

330 **Extension:** Have children draw pictures of their revised predictions.

Level 5/Unit 2
Make, Confirm, or Revise Predictions   2

Macmillan/McGraw-Hill

MAKE A STORY

Character— Tells Who	Setting— Tells Where	Plot— Tells What
Sam the spaceman	a zoo	wins a race
Liza the lizard	a castle	loses a tooth
King Alfred	a city	finds a gold egg
Daisy the donkey	a school	wins a race

Make up your own story. Choose a character, a setting, and a plot. Give your story a title. Write at least four sentences.

_____

_____

_____

_____

_____

_____

Level 5/Unit 2
**ANALYZE STORY ELEMENTS: Character,
Plot, Setting**

4

Extension: Invite children to share their stories with the class.

331

Macmillan/McGraw-Hill

WHAT'S MY JOB?

Use the pictures and sentences to figure out the meaning of the underlined word. Circle the answer.

1. Anna went to the store. She bought new shoes.
   She paid the cashier. A cashier is a person who

   > takes money in a store.
   > takes care of animals.
   > fixes cars.

2. The florist helped Karen pick out flowers to buy.
   She put them in a vase and wrapped them up.
   A florist is a person who

   > sells bread.
   > sells flowers.
   > sells computers.

3. The carpenter built a shed. He cut the boards.
   He nailed the boards together. A carpenter is a
   person who

   > makes pottery.
   > makes clothes.
   > makes things from wood.

4. Which one could build a house? Circle 1 2 3

332 **Extension:** Have children choose one of the occupations and write a list of questions they have about it.

Level 5/Unit 2
CONTEXT CLUES: Unfamiliar Words   4

Macmillan/McGraw-Hill

A LETTER TO AMY

Read each question. Fill in the circle in front of the answer.

I. Who did Peter write a letter to?
  ○ his mother   ○ the boys   ○ Amy

2. Why did Peter write the letter?
  ○ to tell the boys about a camping trip
  ○ to invite Amy to his birthday party
  ○ to tell his mother about a meeting at school

3. When was Peter's party?
  ○ Friday at 3   ○ Tuesday at 5   ○ Saturday at 2

4. What happened to the letter when Peter went to mail it?
  ○ The wind blew it out of Peter's hand.
  ○ Peter lost the letter.
  ○ Peter left the letter at home.

5. How did Amy get the letter?
  ○ Peter handed it to her.
  ○ Peter mailed it to her.
  ○ Peter's mother brought it to Amy's house.

6. Who did Peter bump into when he was chasing the letter?
  ○ Amy   ○ the boys   ○ a dog

Extension: Encourage children to discuss Peter's mixed-up feelings about inviting Amy to his birthday party.

Macmillan/McGraw-Hill

MAKE A WORD

Look at each picture. Write a letter or letters from the box that complete each picture name.

p	n	s	tr	m	sn

1. _____ ail

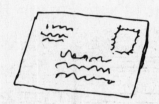

2. _____ ail

3. _____ ail

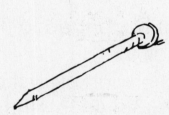

4. _____ ail

5. _____ ail

6. _____ ail

334   **Extension:** Have children make up sentences using the **-ail** words.

Level 5/Unit 2
Long Vowels and Phonograms /ā/ -ail   6

Macmillan/McGraw-Hill

TEST YOUR SKILLS

Circle the word that names the picture.

1. 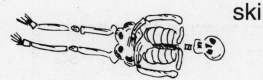   ski   scarf   skeleton

2.    sky   school   skunk

3.   skirt   skip   school

4. 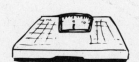   skate   scale   ski

5.    skunk   scooter   skin

6.    sky   scarf   scooter

Macmillan/McGraw-Hill

6

Level 5/Unit 2
Consonant Blends /sk/ *sk, sc, sch*

Extension: Have children draw pictures of some of the words they did not circle.

335

UNIT VOCABULARY REVIEW

Look at the words in the box. Underline the word your teacher says.

1. storm string store	**2.** crayons crowd carrots	**3.** envelope everyone empty
4. special present smell	**5.** attic apples against	**6.** fur before final
7. breakfast birthday basket	**8.** party paint picture	**9.** stamp store string
10. chew shoes share	**11.** before board breakfast	**12.** secret everyone someone
13. board crowd hard	**14.** smell sniff special	**15.** carrots fruit final

Macmillan/McGraw-Hill